max / a play

By the same author

The Tin Drum

Cat and Mouse

Dog Years

Selected Poems

The Plebeians Rehearse the Uprising

Four Plays

New Poems

Speak Out!

Local Anaesthetic

max / a play by günter grass

Translated by A. Leslie Willson and Ralph Manheim

An Original Harvest Book

A Helen and Kurt Wolff Book

Harcourt Brace Jovanovich, Inc., New York

Originally published in Germany in *Theaterspiele* by
Günter Grass, under the title *Davor*

Copyright © 1970 by Hermann Luchterhand Verlag,
Neuwied und Berlin
English translation copyright © 1972
by Harcourt Brace Jovanovich, Inc.

ISBN 0-15-657782-8
Library of Congress Catalog Card Number: 70-178590
Printed in the United States of America

cast of characters

EBERHARD STARUSCH, *a teacher*

IRMGARD SEIFERT, *a teacher*

THE DENTIST

PHILIPP SCHERBAUM, *called Flip, a student*

VERONIKA LEWAND, *called Vero, a student*

[*The open stage reveals all acting areas simultaneously. Differences in level keep the areas separate. Entrances and exits are made possible by screens. It is the author's wish that all directors should forgo film fade-ins, night-club acts, and mass scenes intended to demonstrate something that the author does not wish to demonstrate. The props are to be used economically and leave room for the play. The range of style in the dialogue varies; it is direct, indirect, in spite of a partner partnerless; it is carried on close up or at a distance. The reality is stage reality*]

STARUSCH [*in the dentist's chair*]:
Tell me, Doc, what do you really think of the Soviet system?

DENTIST [*next to the chair*]:
What is needed is a worldwide, socially integrated sick-care plan.—Rinse again, please.

STARUSCH [*takes the glass*]:
But in what system is your sick-care plan supposed to . . .

DENTIST:
In place of all previous systems it is supposed to . . .

STARUSCH:

But isn't your sick-care plan itself a system? [*He rinses*]

DENTIST:

Global sick care has nothing to do with any ideology, it is the basis and superstructure of our human society.

STARUSCH:

But a sick-care plan is only for sick people.

DENTIST:

Keep rinsing, please.—Everybody is sick, was sick, gets sick, dies.

STARUSCH:

But what's the use of all that, if no system educates man to surpass himself?

DENTIST:

What good are systems that prevent man from finding out what ails him?

STARUSCH:

But if we want to get rid of human failings . . .

DENTIST:

Then get rid of human beings.—But now let's . . .

STARUSCH:

I don't want to rinse anymore.

DENTIST:

Think of your porcelain bridges.

STARUSCH [*rinses briefly*]:

But how can we change the world without a system?

DENTIST:

Once we do away with systems, it will be changed.

4

STARUSCH:

Who's going to do away with them? [*He rinses*]

DENTIST:

The sick people. Then at last there will be room for the all-embracing Global Sick-Care Plan, which won't govern us but will care for us, which won't change us but will help us, which—as Seneca remarked—will give us leisure for our infirmities.

STARUSCH:

Ah, the whole world a hospital . . .

DENTIST:

. . . with no more healthy people and no obligation to be healthy.

STARUSCH:

But where does that leave my pedagogical principle?

DENTIST:

Just as you want to do away with the difference between teachers and students, we will abolish the difference between doctor and patient once and for all —we'll do it systematically.

STARUSCH:

Do it systematically.

DENTIST:

But now let's put in the bridges.

STARUSCH:

Put in the bridges.

DENTIST:

Your tongue will soon get used to the foreign bodies.

STARUSCH:

Foreign bodies.

[The DENTIST *gets to work.* SCHERBAUM *and* VERO LEWAND *enter with their bicycles]*

SCHERBAUM:

When Old Hardy had to submit to dental treatment, he said to us: Please show consideration for your poor teacher.

VERO LEWAND *[laughs]*:

He's suffering.—Saint Apollonia, pray for him!
*[*SCHERBAUM *demonstrates the procedure on* VERO LEWAND*]*

SCHERBAUM:

When Apollonia, the patron saint of all who suffer from toothache, was burned in Alexandria in the year 250, the mob first pulled all her teeth with pliers and similar instruments.

VERO LEWAND *[mimics the saint, yells]*:

Ow, ow! Ogod, Ogod—But I still say: No student co-responsibility without student co-determination.

BOTH *[repeating softly in rhythm]*:

No SCR without SCD.
*[*IRMGARD SEIFERT *enters]*

IRMGARD SEIFERT *[next to an aquarium]*:

Maybe I ought to change the water. *[She feeds the tropical fish]*

VERO LEWAND:

What about our smoking corner next to the bicycle shed?

SCHERBAUM:

Let them edit their lousy sheet themselves.

VERO LEWAND:
If you don't do it, somebody else will.

IRMGARD SEIFERT:
If only something would happen. If anything at all would happen. [*Exits*]

DENTIST:
So, my friend, the bridges in your lower jaw fit.

SCHERBAUM:
I'd rather do something else, something relevant that will be a sensation.

VERO LEWAND:
But look: With the magazine we'd have a springboard.

SCHERBAUM [*jumps up*]:
And I'll do it by myself, too.

DENTIST:
You held out like a Stoic.

SCHERBAUM:
I'll do it.
[*He and* VERO LEWAND *take their bicycles out of the racks*]

DENTIST:
Now a week's rest period.

SCHERBAUM:
They'll toss their cookies.

VERO LEWAND:
Do the magazine instead, Flip.
[*Both jump onto their bikes, ride in a circle*]

DENTIST:
>   And as soon as we've recovered, we'll attend to the
>   upper jaw.

STARUSCH [*gets up from the dentist's chair*]:
>   Kind of short, a week.

DENTIST:
>   And here are two tablets for the road. [*Hands him a
>   glass and tablets*]

VERO LEWAND:
>   If you're editor-in-chief, we can expose the whole
>   business. Mao says . . .

SCHERBAUM:
>   Teeny bopper.

VERO LEWAND:
>   Say that again!

SCHERBAUM [*amiably*]:
>   Teeny bopper.
>   [*Both ride off laughing*]

STARUSCH [*swallows the tablets*]:
>   You see, there's a lot of unfinished business at
>   school.

DENTIST:
>   Appointments are available in two weeks as well.

STARUSCH:
>   I've got to get busy with my seniors.

DENTIST [*holds a hand mirror before* STARUSCH]:
>   What do you say, now?

STARUSCH [*startled*]:
>   Great, Doc. Just great.

DENTIST:

You could get into the movies with those.

STARUSCH:

They want Scherbaum to take over the student magazine, but he's refused.

DENTIST:

And when you come again, I'll show you some documentation. In spite of prophylaxis, decay is marching ahead.

STARUSCH:

Even if it is contrary to pedagogical principles, Scherbaum is my favorite student.

DENTIST:

Especially the decay of milk teeth, terrifying, simply terrifying. [*Shows him an x-ray film*]

STARUSCH [*holding the film up to the light*]:

You ought to meet the youngster sometime. Extremely gifted!

DENTIST:

Here and here you see how it spreads in the fissures and on the smooth surfaces.

STARUSCH [*hands back the film*]:

Extremely gifted, Doc. But I don't want to keep you any longer . . . [*Takes his coat*]

DENTIST:

Your rather overtaxed gums have a tendency to inflammation. Call me if anything comes up. [*Hands him a prescription*] The family size ought to carry you through.
[*He exits. In his coat* STARUSCH *slowly goes to center stage. Later he sits down at his school desk*]

．．．

STARUSCH:

It means something to be a teacher. Something is expected of a teacher. We expect something more of a teacher. The teacher as such. He sits in a glass house and corrects papers. [*Lecturing*] However, there is no meaning in history, only organized chaos.—Why are you smiling, Scherbaum?

SCHERBAUM:

Because that doesn't stop you from teaching, or from looking for a meaning in history.—Meaningless history is just something you can't take. [*He takes his bicycle, rides away*]

STARUSCH:

What should I do? Run out of the classroom? Take a stand on the playground and yell: Stop! Stop! That's all wrong! O.K., I don't know what's right, but this has got to stop! stop!
[SCHERBAUM *enters with his bicycle, over to* STARUSCH]

SCHERBAUM:

Excuse me. I've got to talk to you. It's urgent.

STARUSCH:

I've just come from the dentist. Is it really pressing?

SCHERBAUM:

It can wait till tomorrow. But it's urgent all right. [*Jumps on his bike, rides in circles around Starusch*]

STARUSCH:

I like this student. He makes me uneasy. What does he want? What can wait till tomorrow?

SCHERBAUM [*from the bike*]:

I'll do it.

STARUSCH:

Is he going to reform the student magazine, after all?

SCHERBAUM:

You can't reform an absurdity.

STARUSCH:

I assume you want to take over the editorship.

SCHERBAUM [*climbs off the bike*]:

You believe in reformed absurdity—not me. I've got a plan.

STARUSCH:

Maybe emigrate?

SCHERBAUM:

And I'll do it, too.

STARUSCH:

May I ask precisely what?

SCHERBAUM:

I'm going to burn my dog.

STARUSCH:

You don't say.

SCHERBAUM:

On the Avenue. In the afternoon.

STARUSCH:

I thought you had something important to tell me.

SCHERBAUM:

Outside the terrace restaurant at the Hotel Kempinski, at the rush hour.

11

STARUSCH:

Interesting. And why there of all places?

SCHERBAUM:

Give the ladies with the cloche hats something to look at.

STARUSCH:

If you want to shock old ladies, there are plenty of ways; besides, a dog's not for burning.

SCHERBAUM:

Neither are people.

STARUSCH:

You've got something there.—But why a dog?

SCHERBAUM:

Because Berliners are crazy about dogs.

STARUSCH:

Fine, Philipp. But even seeing it your way: a dog isn't so easy to burn.

SCHERBAUM:

I'll douse him with gasoline.

STARUSCH:

But an animal . . . We're talking about an animal . . .

SCHERBAUM:

No trouble getting the gas. I'll notify the press and the T.V. people, and paint a placard: This is gasoline, not napalm. That's what I want them to see. And when he's burning, Max'll run toward the tables with the cakes on 'em. Maybe something'll catch fire. Then maybe they'll understand.

STARUSCH:

What do you want them to understand?

SCHERBAUM:

Well, what it is to burn.

STARUSCH:

They'll kill you.

SCHERBAUM:

That's possible.

STARUSCH:

It that what you want?

SCHERBAUM:

No.

[*He jumps onto his bike and is about to ride off.*
VERO LEWAND *comes toward him on her bike. Both
ride in a circle.* STARUSCH *goes to the desk*]

STARUSCH:

Telephone. Call somebody, anybody.

[*Dials a number. The* DENTIST *enters, puts his hand
on the receiver*]

He tells me that on the playground. And then leaves
me standing there.

VERO LEWAND:

Got a moment, Flip?

SCHERBAUM:

No time.

STARUSCH:

Should we take it seriously?

DENTIST:

First of all let's get this straight: Something has got
to happen.

VERO LEWAND:

This evening we're discussing surplus value.

13

SCHERBAUM:

I'll be busy with my shorthand, late bourgeois.

DENTIST:

Then let's ask ourselves: Why has something got
to happen?

STARUSCH:

Something has got to happen because nothing is
happening.

VERO LEWAND:

Come on.

SCHERBAUM:

Groups stink.

DENTIST:

And what does Seneca say about games in the
arena?
[*Both ride off laughing*]

DENTIST [*quotes*]:

Is there an intermission?—Let them slit people's
throats in the meantime, then at least something
will be happening.—Fire is a similar gap-filler.

STARUSCH:

But we're talking about my student . . .

DENTIST:

You said that before.—And how do we feel other-
wise? Has the inflammation subsided? I forgot to
advise you not to drink anything too cold or eat anything too hot because despite the layer of quartz
cement the metal in our bridges is still a conductor.
—And by the way: Public burnings are not a deterrent, they merely satisfy a craving.

14

STARUSCH:

I'll tell that to Scherbaum. I'll tell that to Scherbaum.—By the way, your report yesterday, excellent.

IRMGARD SEIFERT:

But still unsatisfactory, my dear colleague. Despite the structural improvements: Don't you have the feeling, too, that something has to happen, has to happen as a matter of principle? [*She exits*]

STARUSCH:

Go ahead and do it: If nobody does it, everything will go on as before. I would have done it when I was seventeen. When I think of the things . . . It was wartime then. It's always wartime. Do it. There are plenty of arguments against it. Do it for me. For me it's too late. At forty a man always has to say: Better not, Scherbaum . . .
[SCHERBAUM *enters with his bicycle*]
Listen: Public burnings are not a deterrent, they merely satisfy cravings.

SCHERBAUM:

That's right about burning humans; but the Berliners won't be able to take a burning dog.

STARUSCH:

Think of the newspapers, the *Morning Post*.

SCHERBAUM:

So what? That's old stuff.

STARUSCH:

A coward, they'll say. Let him douse himself, if he wants to show what napalm is like.

SCHERBAUM:

You just said that burnings satisfy cravings.

STARUSCH:

I still say so. Let's just think back: The cruel contests in the Roman arena. Seneca says . . .

SCHERBAUM:

Max is the only thing left. A burning dog, that'll get 'em. Nothing else will. They can read about it all day, and peer at pictures with a magnifying glass or be right there with T.V. They'll only say: Terrible, terrible. But when my dog burns, they'll toss their cookies.

[*Pause.* VERO LEWAND *rides past on her bike and around both of them*]

STARUSCH:

Now just listen, Scherbaum . . .

VERO LEWAND:

I hear a wheedling voice . . . A little appeaser called Old Hardy . . .

STARUSCH:

. . . in the war, I mean in the last one . . .

VERO LEWAND:

Watch out, Flip!

STARUSCH:

. . . in my home town, a submarine tender was set on fire by saboteurs . . .

16

VERO LEWAND:

Now comes the old historical objectivity.

STARUSCH:

The crew—all midshipmen and naval cadets—tried to leave the ship through the portholes.

VERO LEWAND:

So what!

STARUSCH:

They burned up from inside because their hip bones got stuck. Well, don't you see? Or in Hamburg, for example, where the phosphorus bombs set fire to the asphalt streets. Water was no use. And the people who ran out of their houses ran onto the burning asphalt streets.
[VERO LEWAND *climbs off her bike, listens*]
They covered them with sand to keep the air out. But as soon as the air got in again they went on burning. Today no one can imagine what burning alive is like.—Do you follow me?

SCHERBAUM:

Perfectly. And because nobody can imagine that, I have to take Max to the Avenue—in the afternoon.

VERO LEWAND:

Come on, Flip. Old Hardy will never get it.

STARUSCH:

Just a minute, Scherbaum. A few days ago you were offered the editorship of the student magazine.

VERO LEWAND:

So what! [*Laughs*] Anybody can do that kid stuff.

SCHERBAUM:

You stay out of this.—I don't care whether, when, or where students smoke.

STARUSCH:

I know what you mean. But wouldn't it be a magnificent challenge to transform that worthless sheet into a serious forum which—quite apart from the controversial smoking corner and similar student causes—could also discuss the Vietnam question with complete frankness, and even with pro and con columns.

VERO LEWAND:

You can't pre-empt Flip.

STARUSCH:

But you're interested in enlightenment, aren't you?

SCHERBAUM:

You can't mean that seriously. You're just saying that because you're a teacher. It's too late for that.
[SCHERBAUM *and* VERO LEWAND *leave* STARUSCH *standing, exit*]

STARUSCH:

St. Apollonia, pray for me. [*At the telephone, dials*] Yes. The inflammation has subsided. It's about Scherbaum. He's quite capable of doing it. Should I report him? Should I, I of all people, report . . . I'd rather . . . [*Hangs up*]

DENTIST:

All right, keep talking. And write this on the blackboard: He's still talking, so he's not doing anything.

BLACKOUT

scene two

[STARUSCH *sits in one corner of the couch*, IRMGARD
SEIFERT *in the other*]

IRMGARD SEIFERT:

I'm glad you have time for me. I'm at the end of my
tether. Literally at the end.

STARUSCH:

I feel the same way.

IRMGARD SEIFERT:

Remember? Two weeks ago I went to see my mother
in Hanover. After lunch I was rummaging around
in our attic and quite by chance I found these letters
in a wicker trunk, here . . . [*She takes a bundle of
letters from her purse*]

STARUSCH:

You told me. You wrote them when you were seventeen, didn't you, just before the end of the war?
Scherbaum is seventeen, too . . .

IRMGARD SEIFERT:

Yes, I was seventeen, but I was already responsible,
I was deputy leader of a children's evacuation center in the Harz Mountains. And what did I do: In
my drunken, hysterical hopes of victory I was
thoughtless enough to have thirteen- to fourteen-
year-old boys instructed in the firing of the bazooka.

STARUSCH:

It's just such ignorant thoughtlessness that I have in mind when I point out that Scherbaum, too, is only seventeen . . .

IRMGARD SEIFERT:

I know that you have my interest at heart. But this can't be whitewashed by a parallel with some bit of schoolboy foolishness. I informed on a farmer in Clausthal-Zellerfeld just because he refused to let us dig a tank trap in his turnip patch. There. Read them.

STARUSCH [*brushes them aside*]:

You've told me about it, many times. Anyway, the authorities didn't follow up your denunciation.

IRMGARD SEIFERT:

That has nothing to do with it.

STARUSCH:

It has a great deal to do with it. Nothing happened to the farmer.

IRMGARD SEIFERT:

That's a frivolous argument. My intention was to . . .

STARUSCH:

Your intention was the stupidity of a typical Nazi brat. If there's any point in these letters today, it's probably this: that your belated insight ought to sharpen your understanding for the problems of to-day's seventeen-year-olds. [*Pause*]

IRMGARD SEIFERT:

Maybe you're right. Sometimes I have hopes that these young people will *do* something—but nothing happens.

[STARUSCH *stands up, holds his cheek.* IRMGARD SEIFERT *is smoking*]

STARUSCH:

What does she expect? Salvation in her lifetime? There's no such thing. There's only tablets specially prepared for aching teeth and jaws. [*He takes two tablets*] It hurts, my dear Scherbaum, it hurts. [SCHERBAUM *enters with his bike, remains in the background*]

SCHERBAUM:

You and your toothaches. And what's going on out there? In the Mekong Delta? Have you read about that?

STARUSCH:

Yes, Scherbaum, I *have* read about it. It's bad. Bad-bad. But I must admit that I am more stricken, exposed, and robbed of all sense and security by this aching, this stream of air always aimed at the same nerve, and this throbbing, this localized, regular ache, which isn't actually so bad and is easily deadened by anaesthetic, than by the sum of horrible columns of figures, than by the photographed, immense, and still abstract ache of this world—because it doesn't touch my nerve.

SCHERBAUM:

But doesn't it make you mad, or at least sad?

STARUSCH:

I often *try* to be sad.

SCHERBAUM:

Aren't you enraged by injustice out there and everywhere?

STARUSCH:

I always make an effort to be enraged.

SCHERBAUM:

I mean . . .

STARUSCH:

So do I.

[SCHERBAUM *exits with his bike*]

IRMGARD SEIFERT:

Do believe me, my dear colleague. Something is going to happen. This new, unburdened generation will put an end to all that antiquated mischief.

STARUSCH [*laughs*]:

They're wishing and longing for something. Just look at us: How skeptical the war left us precocious children. How alert we were going to be, how mistrustful of grown-ups. What's left of all that? Settled citizens in their mid-thirties and forties hardly find time to remember their defeats. We've learned to fight our way through. To feel out the situation. To use our elbows. To conform if necessary. We're practical people, we aim for goals and—when no unexpected obstacles arise—actually achieve them. But that's about all.

IRMGARD SEIFERT:

Undoubtably our generation failed. But our elders . . . wasn't it a convenient evasion to set their hopes in us. To expect deliverance from us? Already marked by a criminal system at seventeen, we couldn't turn the tide, no, we couldn't . . . couldn't . . .

[*The* DENTIST *enters*]

. . .

STARUSCH [*softly*]:

A new era. Redemption. Deliverance. Purification.
Sacrifice.

DENTIST:

All white elephants . . . which have recently been
finding customers. But tooth decay is marching on.

IRMGARD SEIFERT:

We had given up before laying the first stone.

DENTIST:

What we lack is comprehensive prophylaxis at the
pre-school age. [*Points to charts*] These figures speak
for themselves.

IRMGARD SEIFERT:

Now they'll sweep us aside.

STARUSCH:

Who's going to sweep us aside?

IRMGARD SEIFERT:

The new, the unprecedented. The coming generation.

DENTIST:

We still know too little.

STARUSCH:

When I think of Scherbaum . . .

IRMGARD SEIFERT:

And still I thought I was doing the right thing when
I tried to destroy an enemy in that farmer . . .
[VERO LEWAND *and* SCHERBAUM *enter*]

SCHERBAUM:

You are still collecting, aren't you?

DENTIST:

We cling to error.

STARUSCH:

My own doubt is enough for me.

DENTIST:

No lacto bacillus.

VERO LEWAND:

When'll it be, Flip, when?

SCHERBAUM:

I've brought you something. Here. [*He offers her two Mercedes stars*]

IRMGARD SEIFERT:

That's guilt, Eberhard. Guilt, no doubt about it.

DENTIST:

It would be desirable to . . .

IRMGARD SEIFERT:

And this guilt must be articulated . . .

DENTIST:

. . . change the microflora in the oral cavity.

IRMGARD SEIFERT:

. . . or kept silent.

VERO LEWAND:

So tell me, Flip, when? [*She takes the Mercedes stars*]

STARUSCH:

Let's drop it.

DENTIST:

But we still don't know in what way the microflora ought to be changed . . .

24

SCHERBAUM:
   I'll manage it.

DENTIST:
   . . . in order to provide an effective prophylaxis against tooth decay.
   [DENTIST, VERO LEWAND, *and* SCHERBAUM *exit*]

IRMGARD SEIFERT:
   Yes, let's drop it.—By the way, your rug is pretty.

STARUSCH:
   A new acquisition.

IRMGARD SEIFERT:
   Persian, isn't it?

STARUSCH:
   What I was about to say: In line with your report on the new Berlin model consolidated school, which I found really excellent—[*Sits down next to her on the couch*]—don't you think that the Hamburg attempt at an integrated school also deserves our special attention, particularly because it will help to get rid of the obsolete forms of entrance examinations and promotion requirements . . . [*Takes her hand*]

IRMGARD SEIFERT:
   Look, Eberhard, look at these letters. For years I believed I had always been against it. I'll have to quit teaching.

BLACKOUT

scene three

[SCHERBAUM *and* VERO LEWAND *with their bicycles on the stage apron.* SCHERBAUM *points at the audience*]

SCHERBAUM:
There they sit, shoveling it in.

VERO LEWAND:
The hats they wear, like pots.

SCHERBAUM:
They're thinking only of cream pies, nothing else.

VERO LEWAND:
What do they talk about, when they talk?

SCHERBAUM:
Oh, about weight and reducing.

VERO LEWAND:
They look really stuffed.

SCHERBAUM:
Just look at the cake forks.

VERO LEWAND:
And the way they crook their little fingers.

SCHERBAUM:
They've all got at least three pounds of jewelry.

VERO LEWAND:
Ugh. You can smell 'em all the way over here.

SCHERBAUM:

Cake-eating fur-bearing animals.

VERO LEWAND:

That's Persian lamb. My mother has one, too. Look at that one—the way she's gobbling.—Where do you plan to do it?

SCHERBAUM:

Here, right here.

VERO LEWAND:

So far away?

SCHERBAUM:

I figured it out—the field of vision and all that.

VERO LEWAND:

It's . . .

SCHERBAUM:

. . . enough to make you puke. Say it: to make you puke.
[*Both laugh*]

VERO LEWAND:

So when'll it be, Flip? Tomorrow?

SCHERBAUM:

When I told Old Hardy about it yesterday, he had a couple of arguments up his sleeve, of course.

VERO LEWAND:

Him? He'd better stay out of it. Him and his stories about what he was like at seventeen. All he does is talk.

SCHERBAUM:

As a teacher that's all he can do.

VERO LEWAND:

Just look how they're gawking!

SCHERBAUM:

If we can't convince Old Hardy, how are we going to make those cake-eating hats . . .

VERO LEWAND:

Do it, Flip. Do it soon.

SCHERBAUM:

So they'll know what it's like . . .
[*Climbs on his bike. The* DENTIST *and* STARUSCH *enter*]

VERO LEWAND:

Are you coming today?
[STARUSCH *dials*]

SCHERBAUM [*riding*]:

. . . to run around in flames.

VERO LEWAND [*riding after him*]:

We're doing base and superstructure.

SCHERBAUM [*riding in a circle with* VERO LEWAND]:

I've got shorthand.

VERO LEWAND:

You're going on with that?
[SCHERBAUM *and* VERO LEWAND *exit. The* DENTIST *and* STARUSCH *hang up*]

STARUSCH:

I told him fine just now when he asked how I felt, though my gums hurt and I have to rinse every four hours.

DENTIST:

Teachers always remind us of teachers we've
had . . .

STARUSCH:

Then I developed my plan, which he called a typical
teacher's plan . . .

DENTIST:

. . . or of teachers in books, who are said to be
reminiscent of other teachers.

STARUSCH:

. . . and then he gave me practical advice, as if he
were talking about a root treatment.

DENTIST:

Dentists, on the other hand, hardly ever appear in
literature.

STARUSCH:

But my material is complete. [*Rolls the projector to
the footlights*]

DENTIST:

At the most in spy novels: the microfilm in the
porcelain bridge. [*Takes a slide tray, goes center
stage*]

STARUSCH:

I almost believe my own arguments.

DENTIST:

We're not interesting, we work too unobtrusively
and painlessly. [*Helps* STARUSCH *turn the projector
with the lens toward the audience*] Local anaesthetic prevents us from being characters.

STARUSCH:

In the state film archives and in the archives of one

of the leading news magazines, I found some black-and-white and some color slides which I should like to project for Scherbaum in the biology lecture hall. [SCHERBAUM *enters*]

DENTIST:

My lecture series at the Tempelhof Adult Education Center is moderately to poorly attended.

SCHERBAUM:

I can just imagine what you're going to dish up.

DENTIST:

Who is going to listen when I warn them about tooth decay?

STARUSCH:

As long as you've told me about your absurd plan, you at least ought to give me—your teacher—a chance.

SCHERBAUM:

All right. So that afterwards you, my teacher, can tell yourself that you tried everything.

DENTIST:

Tooth decay is an ailment of civilization. [*He operates the projector from the left*] Among the Polynesian islanders with their primitive way of life we find only a .32 per cent incidence of caries, while among the civilized inhabitants of those same islands a 21.9 per cent incidence of caries has been recorded.

STARUSCH [*operates the projector from the right*]:

First, a woodcut featuring the burning of witches and Jews in the Middle Ages. By the way, at witch-burnings particular kinds of wood were pre-ferred . . .

DENTIST:

And here on the left the microflora of the saliva of caries-free test subjects . . .

STARUSCH:

Willow, for example, and freshly cut gorse because of the greenish smoke.

DENTIST:

. . . and on the right the carious focus in decay-afflicted test subjects.

STARUSCH:

Now boiling in oil for the mortification of the lust-ful flesh.

DENTIST:

Here you see enamel and dentine caries.

STARUSCH:

Now the burning of John Hus.—Now the burning of natives by the Spaniards in South and Central America.—And now the burning of widows in India . . .

DENTIST:

And here the incidence of caries among individual pre-school age groups from the twenty-fifth to the seventy-eighth month.

STARUSCH:

What do you think, Scherbaum?—We ought to have a general discussion of burnt offerings some time. Now documentary pictures: The effects of the early flame throwers.

DENTIST:

Here South Swedish and Hungarian data on the incidence of caries of the milk teeth.

STARUSCH:

It's not just the Bible that provides particulars.—These are phosphorus burns inflicted in the Second World War.—Now Dresden. Please note the shriveled, stacked-up corpses.

DENTIST:

As these tables show, the food restrictions imposed during the last two world wars definitely reduced the incidence of caries.

STARUSCH:

Finally, the self-immolation of a Vietnamese nun.

DENTIST:

So even war can have its advantages.

STARUSCH:

Well, Philipp? So quiet?

DENTIST:

Next time I shall speak about the harmlessness of sweets. But let me say this in closing: If there were fewer politicians and more dentists, the world would be better off. The world would be a little better off.

[*He exits.* STARUSCH *packs up his slides*]

SCHERBAUM [*with crossed arms*]:

That was just people. This is going to be a dog, don't you see? Human beings, everybody knows that. Everybody's accepted it. Like in the Middle Ages, that's what they say. But a living dog, here in Berlin . . .

STARUSCH:

You're wrong, Scherbaum. Think of the pigeons. Poisoned. By the thousands. Operation Grand, they called it. Right here, in Berlin.

SCHERBAUM:

Sure. But that was a mass action. They were a nuisance and had to be gotten rid of. It was planned and publicized. Everybody had time to look the other way. That made it all right.

STARUSCH:

What are you talking about, Scherbaum?

SCHERBAUM:

The massacre of the pigeons. [*Pause.* STARUSCH *nods, as though he were about to say: "Of course, of course"*] —I also know that they used to set rats on fire to get rid of rats. I've also heard of incendiaries starting fires with blazing chickens. But a burning running howling dachshund, in a city like Berlin, that's crazy about dogs—that's something new. Only when a dog burns will they catch on that the Yanks are burning people over there—doing it every day.

STARUSCH [*absent-mindedly*]:

Sure, sure.—But about that job as editor-in-chief, I still think you ought to . . . But you don't want to, of course.

SCHERBAUM [*places the cover over the projector*]:

Well, many thanks anyway. It was really very interesting.

[*He leaves* STARUSCH *standing, exits.* STARUSCH *pushes the projector back. The* DENTIST *enters*]

. . .

DENTIST:

> I'm sorry to hear it. But we won't give up. Does your student show any signs of pity for the dog?

STARUSCH [*reflects*]:

> Yes. Yes, indeed. Yesterday Scherbaum and his dachshund took me to the bus stop. And he pleaded with me not to believe that the thing with Max— that's the dog's name—left him cold.

DENTIST:

> Then there's still hope.

STARUSCH:

> I only hope the young man comes down with a good case of the flu.

DENTIST:

> Even that is hope. Even that. [*Laughs*] —But you know, I've got a patient here . . . You've still got plenty of pills?
> [*Exits.* STARUSCH *takes two tablets*]

STARUSCH:

> Yes. I've got plenty of pills. [*Pause*] That young man is ruining his life. And he's ruining me. What will I look like, if he does it? As if I wouldn't want to. Get in there. Demolish. Ten thousand bull-dozers to clear away the mountains of consumer goods . . . Clear the air. The primal revolutionary urge right after tooth-brushing, just before break-fast. Down with the hypocritical reformists, let the hot breath of revolution blow. Start over again from scratch. [*Begins to rinse*]—This would be a good time for a school trip. [*Rinses*] To Bonn, for instance. [*Rinses*] We could sit in the gallery and hear what they have to say about interim budget

planning. [*Rinses*] And when we get back, themes: How does the parliament operate?—Or: If I were a legislator.—Or provocatively: Parliament or hot-air factory? [*Rinses*] But I could suggest this to Scherbaum: Scherbaum, I advise you not to burn your dog in Berlin, where you'll shock only a few cake-crazed ladies, but in Bonn, the seat of political power.

[SCHERBAUM *and* VERO LEWAND *enter with their bicycles*]

SCHERBAUM:

I've already thought about that myself.

STARUSCH:

Well, then, why here and not in Bonn?

SCHERBAUM:

It would get lost in the general confusion.

VERO LEWAND:

They'd just laugh when they saw Max burning, and they'd say: So what?

STARUSCH:

But Bonn is the seat of power.

VERO LEWAND:

Don't you get it? In Bonn a burning dog is just a public nuisance—in Berlin it will hit them where it hurts.

STARUSCH:

I think you're overestimating the Berliners' feeling for dogs . . .

VERO LEWAND:

A sum total of 53,705 . . .

SCHERBAUM:

A dog for every 32.8 inhabitants.

STARUSCH:

The statistics for registered dogs, like the statistics for the inhabitants of West Berlin, show a recessive tendency.

SCHERBAUM:

I'll stick with Berlin.

STARUSCH:

But in Bonn, only in Bonn . . .

[SCHERBAUM *and* VERO LEWAND *leave him standing there*]

VERO LEWAND:

Old Hardy still believes in his parliament.

SCHERBAUM:

Why doesn't he say: Do it?

VERO LEWAND:

He's a liberal. They twist everything around. If I say cow, they say beef.

[IRMGARD SEIFERT *and the* DENTIST *enter. She feeds the tropical fish*]

IRMGARD SEIFERT:

Anyway, somebody had written on the blackboard: Reactionary cow.

VERO LEWAND:

She's a cow.

DENTIST:

What's going on?

STARUSCH:

My colleague has been called a stupid cow.

VERO LEWAND:
    The Archangel is a cow!

DENTIST:
    Epithets from the dairy farm.

STARUSCH:
    It seems to me her nickname "Archangel" covers it.

IRMGARD SEIFERT:
    Simply ridiculous.

VERO LEWAND:
    I'll stick to cow.

SCHERBAUM:
    Oh cut it out!

IRMGARD SEIFERT:
    I should have removed the barbels after they
    spawned. Now they're eating their own young.

VERO LEWAND:
    Moo!

SCHERBAUM:
    Teeny bopper.
    [SCHERBAUM, VERO LEWAND, *the* DENTIST, *exit.*
    STARUSCH *and* IRMGARD SEIFERT *sit down on the
    couch, keeping their distance*]

IRMGARD SEIFERT:
    Naturally, I didn't bother with that nonsense . . .

STARUSCH:
    So that's the way it is: Scherbaum isn't suffering
    from an obsession . . .

IRMGARD SEIFERT:
    Somehow little Lewand reminds me of myself back
    in my teens . . .

STARUSCH:

   . . . no, it's a deliberate plan that will be carried
out, if not tomorrow then the day after . . .

IRMGARD SEIFERT:

   Since we belong to the same generation, maybe you
can understand me: These old letters have changed
me to the core. [STARUSCH *laughs*] Your laughing
proves it. I've become ridiculous. I've become a
member of a society that can't admit it's ridiculous. So people laugh. So *you* laugh. But I want
you to listen. I insist. It was toward the end of the
war . . .

STARUSCH [*puts his hand on the telephone*]:

   What should I do, Doc?
   [*The* DENTIST *enters*]

DENTIST:

   It's got to take its course.

STARUSCH:

   Now comes the inevitable bazooka.

DENTIST:

   Listen and provide discreet guidance. [*Fills out index cards*]

IRMGARD SEIFERT:

   But that hysterical scream—"Bazookas"—calls my
whole existence into question . . .

STARUSCH:

   Now I'm for that farmer in the Harz.—Who today
would accuse a girl who was seventeen at the time,
when our Chancellor's past . . .

IRMGARD SEIFERT [*violently*]:
I forfeited any right to judge the Kiesinger
case . . .

STARUSCH:
Now, Doc, now.

IRMGARD SEIFERT:
. . . when I reported a simple farmer to Party
headquarters . . .

STARUSCH [*in a rage, trying to stop her*]:
Again I ask you to remember that your report had
no consequences. If you can't do it yourself, I'll
exonerate you.

IRMGARD SEIFERT [*jumping up*]:
I forbid you to try to resolve my problem in such a
superficial way.

STARUSCH:
Then I beg you to forgive my frivolity and help me
figure out how we can help our student Scherbaum.
[*Pause*]

DENTIST:
Anyway, she's shut up.

STARUSCH:
Scherbaum is suffering from the state of the world.
The most distant injustice hits him. He thinks he's
living right next door to the war in Vietnam. He
sees no way out—or only one: He wants to give the
world a sign by burning his dog in public.

IRMGARD SEIFERT [*sharply*]:
That's nonsense.

DENTIST:
I admit it's nonsense.

STARUSCH:

Still, we've got to learn to understand the youngster.

IRMGARD SEIFERT [*emphatically*]:

Irresponsible nonsense! You ought to report him.

STARUSCH:

You think . . .

IRMGARD SEIFERT:

I don't just think. I advise you most emphatically.

DENTIST:

Keep cool now.

STARUSCH:

To the school administration?

IRMGARD SEIFERT:

Pooh! Threaten the boy with the police. Then we'll see. And if you don't want to, I'll have to do it.
[*She exits.* STARUSCH *and the* DENTIST *pick up the telephone receivers*]

DENTIST:

Tsk tsk tsk. Look who wants to call the guardians of law and order.

STARUSCH:

My colleague has a thing about the police. She still has a thing about the police.—Well, what now, Doc? How does your Seneca comment on the present situation?

DENTIST:

If I may advise you as a dentist, that is, as a modern man devoted to the teachings of the Stoa . . . Continue your talks with the young man. Talk prevents action.

40

STARUSCH:

You treat everything like tooth decay.

DENTIST:

Exactly. Prevention's the thing. Prevention. Not revolution, but dental prophylaxis. Not street fights, but control of thumb-sucking. Do you follow me? Campaigns against breathing through the mouth, and blowing exercises for the distal bite. That's the daily situation on the dental front. There's no need for a new ideology. No. We still have no effective curative toothpaste. We still have no Global Sick-Care Plan. But if you don't mind, my patients are . . .

BLACKOUT

[VERO LEWAND *and* SCHERBAUM *are sitting behind the school desk.* IRMGARD SEIFERT *is next to the aquarium*]

IRMGARD SEIFERT:
Two more guppies with their bellies up. And other defeats. And do you know, I was thinking of giving up teaching.

VERO LEWAND:
Flip! When are you going to do it, anyway?

SCHERBAUM:
I'll do it.

VERO LEWAND:
But when?

SCHERBAUM:
When I'm sure.

VERO LEWAND:
But you are sure, Flip.

SCHERBAUM:
Just about.

IRMGARD SEIFERT [*steps in front of the school desk, lecturing*]:
Our topic is: Action as a factor of liberation.

VERO LEWAND [*responds*]:
  Just a year ago I was picking Mercedes stars with a hacksaw.

IRMGARD SEIFERT:
  Resistance, for example, even hopeless res . . .

VERO LEWAND [*sings*]:
  Pick a star, pick a star . . .

IRMGARD SEIFERT:
  When the men of the July 20th Plot went into action . . .

VERO LEWAND [*jumping up*]:
  That was way back when. What about today—now?

IRMGARD SEIFERT:
  When on June 17th the workers of Stalin Allee . . .

VERO LEWAND:
  Holidays! Lousy holidays!

IRMGARD SEIFERT:
  What those men did, however fruitless, gave us back our dignity.

VERO LEWAND:
  Amen!
  [*She and* SCHERBAUM *run off laughing*]

IRMGARD SEIFERT [*left alone*]:
  That's why we question ourselves today, because it's so quiet, so horribly quiet: If only something would happen, something, anything . . .
  [*She exits.* STARUSCH *and the* DENTIST *enter.* STARUSCH *to the desk. The* DENTIST *starts filling out index cards*]

43

. . .

STARUSCH:

Should such an essay be entitled: Talk prevents action?

DENTIST:

I'm busy, but talk away.

STARUSCH:

Inaction as the sum of experience was recommended in his old age by Seneca, who had written Nero's speeches and supplied action with words.

DENTIST:

A genuine over-bite with mesial centric . . .

STARUSCH:

An active dentist can talk. Activists advise inaction.

DENTIST:

Too much action and too many short-sighted triumphs. I'd rather fill out index cards.

STARUSCH:

Could it be that action is active resignation?

DENTIST [*standing up*]:

Look here: Something is trying to grow, it moves a fraction of a millimeter. Then the activist comes along and knocks out the greenhouse window.

STARUSCH:

You deny, then, that fresh air—fresh air—is beneficial?

DENTIST:

Your supposed beneficial action has stopped a process of development that had definitely promising beginnings. [*Sits down again, writes*]

44

STARUSCH:

I remember how you assessed my tartar at first glance: Well, that does look bad. We've got to remove that radically.—What if I compared capitalism to the tartar that had to be removed?

DENTIST [*laughs*]:

Action is evasion. Something has to happen.

STARUSCH:

Isn't your treatment of my prognathism action?

DENTIST:

Know-how plus skill, my dear sir! While the premature pulling of teeth, that mania for creating a hole that won't hurt anymore, is action without know-how: activated stupidity.

STARUSCH:

Then you recommend reason, study, hesitation, hard work, doubt, fresh beginnings, improvement, step-by-step development: A ridiculous procession, two steps forward and one back.

DENTIST:

. . . whereas the activist overleaps slow processes, throws off the ballast of inhibiting knowledge, whereas the activist is lightfooted and lazy: Laziness as the springboard of action.

STARUSCH:

But so is fear: Development, it would seem, can no longer be read off, no needle registers the slight daily progress. Stalled machines and waste motion breathe the proverbial peace of the graveyard, into which my colleague, Frau Seifert, speaks her: "If only something would happen . . ." Calm in the face of mounting deficits. A terrified submissiveness that my student would like to shake up with his action: Fear promotes action.

DENTIST:

Or: Children whistling in the dark. Even the creation of the world, described as mere serialized action, was an anxiety reaction camouflaged as creation. [*Stands up, laughs*] Somebody should have had a talk with the Old Man up there before it was too late, before he took action. You know my thesis: Talk prevents action.

[*Exits.* SCHERBAUM *enters with his briefcase*]

STARUSCH [*going up to* SCHERBAUM]:

—I'm sorry, Scherbaum, I shall have to report you—to the police. You know what that can mean.

SCHERBAUM [*in an ironically solicitous undertone*]:

I'm sure you wouldn't do that to yourself.

STARUSCH:

All the same I've been having to think about how to formulate such a thing in writing.

SCHERBAUM [*laughs*]:

Turn me in? You—turn me in?—That doesn't go with your haircut.

STARUSCH [*confused*]:

Maybe not, Scherbaum, but I'm warning you that you're forcing me to do things that are deeply repugnant to me.

SCHERBAUM:

You have far too much self-respect for that.

STARUSCH [*distraught*]:

What other arguments can I give you? The sense-

46

lessness, the arrogance of your plan? The bestiality, the stupidity, yes, the stupidity! Or will it do any good if I tell you that your irrational act will be applauded by the wrong people for the wrong reasons?

SCHERBAUM [*with a deprecating gesture*]:
I know all that . . .

STARUSCH:
Frau Seifert would say the same thing if she knew about your plan . . .

SCHERBAUM [*after a searching glance*]:
Oh.
[*To* VERO LEWAND, *who enters with her briefcase*]
Old Hardy has been blabbing to the Archangel.

VERO LEWAND:
To her? She can't say a thing. She keeps talking about resistance. It's a duty, she says. [*She parodies Irmgard Seifert's delivery*] Time and again, in our Nation's darkest hours, there have been men who stood up courageously and took action. They set us a sign. They defied injustice.
[*She and* SCHERBAUM *laugh*]

STARUSCH:
It must be admitted that Frau Seifert sometimes indulges in rather anachronistic pathos . . .

SCHERBAUM:
Why don't you say: Do it. Why don't you say: You're right.—Why don't you help me?

STARUSCH [*getting a grip on himself*]:
Scherbaum, my final word: I will get a dog from the Lankwitz Kennel, I'll get him used to me, and then on the exact spot you designate I'll douse him

with gasoline and set him on fire. And I'll display your placard. The press and T.V. will be there. We'll make up a leaflet together, right to the point, about the effects of napalm. After they've arrested me or finished me off one way or another, you and your girl friend can hand it out on the Avenue. O.K.?

[SCHERBAUM *cocks his head, thinks about it.* VERO LEWAND *becomes restless*]

VERO LEWAND:

Mao warns us against the motley scholars.

SCHERBAUM:

You stay out of this.

VERO LEWAND:

Liberalism is the mortal enemy of revolution.

SCHERBAUM [*to* VERO LEWAND]:

All right. We know. [*To* STARUSCH] I'll have to think it over.

STARUSCH:

No, now, Philipp. What do you say?

SCHERBAUM:

I can't decide without Max. [*He leaves* VERO *and* STARUSCH *standing, exits*]

STARUSCH:

Tell me, Vero. Why do you wear green panty-hose?

VERO LEWAND:

The better to hear you with.

BLACKOUT

[DENTIST *on the telephone.* STARUSCH *making the rounds*]

DENTIST [*after prolonged laughter*]:

I see, I see. You want to gain time. Get a dog. Get the dog used to his master. Let Scherbaum's plan go to seed. Maybe something will happen in the meantime. There's always hope for an armistice. Or the Pope will present the world with a new Peace Encyclical: With burning concern . . . [*Laughs*] And the market will react nervously. Not bad, your tactic, not bad.

STARUSCH:

You don't realize that I'm perfectly serious. I certainly don't want to expose the youngster to the risk of being lynched.

DENTIST:

Let's stick to the subject. At the kennel you ought to try for a covered bitch. That way you'll give your student a chance to release you, his secretly respected teacher, from your promise. He'll never expect you to burn an expectant mother.

STARUSCH:

Your cynicism betrays a medical origin.

DENTIST:

I'm only carrying your idea to its logical conclusion. [*The* DENTIST *hangs up, and exits*]

. . .

STARUSCH:

And suppose it falls on me. Suppose he simply says O.K.—That will narrow my choice. I'll just have to go through with it. West Berlin teacher, forty, protests the war in Vietnam by publicly burning a spitz dog . . . But not on the Avenue. I'd rather get back to the Bonn idea.

[*Puts on his coat, walks.* SCHERBAUM *enters with his bicycle*]

SCHERBAUM:

It won't work.

STARUSCH:

May I know the reason, the reasons?

SCHERBAUM:

I admit it: Naturally Max and I are afraid.

STARUSCH:

Let me do it, Philipp. Even if it sounds pretentious at this point. I'm not afraid.

SCHERBAUM:

And that's why it won't work.

STARUSCH:

That's sophistry.

SCHERBAUM:

You can only do such a thing if you're afraid.

STARUSCH:

My reasons for taking this step are basically of a different kind.

SCHERBAUM:

Just what I'm saying: First of all, you don't believe in it, and secondly you're not even afraid.

STARUSCH:

I used to be afraid.

SCHERBAUM:

This much has become clear to me: What a man does without fear doesn't count. You only want to do it to prevent me from doing it. You're a grown-up, all you care about is limiting the damage.

[*Pause*]

STARUSCH:

Then you think that because I'm a grown-up, I've lost my purity and with it my fear. That because I'm impure, I can't make a sacrifice.

SCHERBAUM [*laughs*]:

Sometimes you talk like the Archangel: really pompous. Sacrifice. Why, that's something symbolic. What we want to do has a purpose. But it won't work unless we're afraid.

STARUSCH:

Philipp, when a man's afraid of doing something and does it anyway, he's making a sacrifice. He sacrifices himself by getting the better of himself.

SCHERBAUM:

I suppose so. In any case this thing has to be absolutely pure.

[SCHERBAUM *jumps onto his bike, rides off.* STARUSCH *slowly goes home by a roundabout route. On the way he meets* IRMGARD SEIFERT]

STARUSCH:

Should have used Tide. Before the sacrifice, please use Tide.

IRMGARD SEIFERT:

I've been thinking about that, my dear colleague. You keep suggesting some kind of compromise. And if I've acquainted you with the horrible contents of these letters, then surely I can expect you to spare me your dirty appeasements in the future.

STARUSCH:

But, my dear colleague, your murky case, or rather, your long-since superannuated youthful foolishness . . .

IRMGARD SEIFERT:

That's enough of your ambiguities!

STARUSCH:

And how are your tropical fish? Who's eating whom right now?

IRMGARD SEIFERT:

If there is a solution, it must be absolutely pure and uncompromising. You must see that! [*She exits*]

STARUSCH [*takes two tablets*]:

I, the fearless teacher who is always limiting damage, Eberhard Starusch, with my minor aches masked by tablets. Because I'm afraid of toothaches. —I should have said: Scherbaum, I am afraid— of the dentist, for instance.

[VERO LEWAND *enters*]

VERO LEWAND:

Are you satisfied?

STARUSCH:

I've just been talking to Mrs. Clean.

VERO LEWAND:

And what did you persuade Flip to do?

STARUSCH:

He persuaded me. Pretty soon I'll have to put up with a compulsory bath. [*Laughs*]

VERO LEWAND:

I'm warning you, Old Hardy. If you don't stop demoralizing Flip with your dirty machinations . . .

STARUSCH [*ironically*]:

Well?

VERO LEWAND:

We'll have to count you as a member of the counter-revolutionary camp . . .

STARUSCH:

. . . and simply liquidate me, right?

VERO LEWAND:

We despise Stalinist methods. But your behavior will have consequences, very definite consequences. [*She exits*]

STARUSCH:

The chaste and virtuous Robespierre covertly sired a large progeny.—I tell you, Doc: A new generation is growing up who for all their display of materialism are looking for a new myth. Just watch out. Watch out.

DENTIST [*entering*]:

But if we were to offer this generation the fight against caries as a revolutionary rite culminating in an absolutely caries-free society, what strength, what sacrificial zeal, what shining enthusiasm might be usefully redirected!

[STARUSCH *puts on his coat, takes a drink, and in*

walking comes across a sketchily indicated bar on a raised platform]

STARUSCH:

Oh, how grievous is the contradistinction.

DENTIST:

It's not true, of course, that the likes of us are free from temptations. How often I'd like to just chuck it all.

STARUSCH:

Oh, how in between we are sitting.

DENTIST:

How often—while removing tartar, or as I dandle a porcelain bridge in my palm—I ask myself: What's it all for?

STARUSCH:

Oh, how disintegrating the ache is.

DENTIST:

And my mother often said: You're too involved, Erich. But it has to be a noiseless, world-wide system. We need a sick-care plan. You must realize that! [*Exits*]

STARUSCH [*at the bar*]:

A beer, waiter, a beer! And a thought, not water soluble, one that gives the right-of-way to the blue light, a brand-new one that will radically part the interlocking miasma so that all of us—waiter, a beer!—all of us, including the backward lookers and the stirrers up of dregs, can go home on the freeway, through the banked-up, right left banked-up Red Sea—waiter, my beer!

[VERO LEWAND *enters, sits down next to him at the bar*]

VERO LEWAND:
I thought you'd be either at Reimann's or here.

STARUSCH [*slightly drunk*]:
Since you know my habits, I suppose I may ask what I can order you.

VERO LEWAND:
Anything. A coke and vodka.

STARUSCH:
A new combination.—Waiter, a coke and vodka. —Once, before I had the doubtful pleasure of practicing the teaching profession, I worked in the cement industry. That knocks you over, doesn't it, my girl? I know the working class. The cement workers used to take a shot or two for breakfast, though without coke for a chaser; they preferred several bottles of Nette beer.

VERO LEWAND:
Why don't you leave Flip alone?

STARUSCH:
The Nette is a small river in the Lower Eifel. The best beer was named after it. The Nette winds picturesquely through Germany's largest pumice-mining area.

VERO LEWAND:
I asked you, why don't you let Flip alone?

STARUSCH:
Pumice makes for thirst. Of course, I don't know whether you're interested in pumice or concrete.

VERO LEWAND:

　　You can't corner me.

STARUSCH:

　　Cement is a commercially produced dusty powder.

VERO LEWAND:

　　You lush!

STARUSCH:

　　As far as I know, Fraulein Lewand, you're partial to green panty-hose and call yourself a Marxist. That makes it hard for me to understand your lack of interest in the cement industry. Just between you and me: I too regard myself as a Marxist.

VERO LEWAND:

　　You're a liberal who can't make up his mind.

STARUSCH:

　　That's right. I'm a liberal Marxist who can't make up his mind.—Waiter, a beer!

VERO LEWAND:

　　You talk about Marxism, but you act like a liberal. That's why you're trying to talk Flip into a corner.

STARUSCH:

　　Waiter, my beer!

VERO LEWAND:

　　But you won't succeed.

STARUSCH:

　　Shall we draw straws to see whether you or I . . .

VERO LEWAND:

　　You're trying to divert him with your crappy student magazine . . .

56

STARUSCH:

Dear Veronika Lewand, it's also in your interest that I should call Philipp's attention to the consequences of such a senseless sacrifice.

VERO LEWAND [*softly determined*]:

In *The Foolish Old Man Who Removed the Mountains*, Mao says: "Be resolute, fear no sacrifice and surmount every difficulty to win victory."—That's it. I'll run along now. We're on the threshold of the Third Revolution. The only people who don't know it are a handful of reactionaries.

[*She turns her back on* STARUSCH *and exits*]

STARUSCH:

Waiter, check. [*He tosses out some money and goes slowly home by a roundabout way*] "Oh, how is the gold become dim."—I ought to assign an essay on that quote from Lamentations, or just on the little word "oh"—on Oh yes—Oh, that's it!—and Oh no —on Oh God and cries of oh and woe.—On the aspirated, astonished, angry OH.—On the Oh in Kleist and the ironic Oh in Thomas Mann.—On the Oh of children and the Oh of feeble old men.—In what way does the Oh for a particularly successful sunset differ from the Oh at the sight of the ocean? —The Oh in the song: Oh I have lost her . . . And the Oh in politics: Oh my dear colleague Barzel . . . Naturally, the Oh in commercials: Oh, I see you wash with Tide . . . And the Oh of women. The Oh-oh-oh-oh . . . I wonder if Philipp already knows about that?

BLACKOUT

[VERO LEWAND *and* SCHERBAUM]

SCHERBAUM:
I won't be able to do it with Max.

VERO LEWAND:
Why not practice up? Try this one, Flip. You can have him. [*Tosses him a stuffed dog*]

SCHERBAUM:
What for? [*Tosses the stuffed dog back*]

VERO LEWAND:
To douse and set on fire. Then you'll be sure. Let's go somewhere, to Glienicke or someplace, and practice.

SCHERBAUM [*irritated*]:
What for?

VERO LEWAND:
To make sure it works. When you get to work with the gasoline, Max will go crazy. Now watch: You pour the bottle over him. I'll pull, as if he were running away. And now with a match or a lighter or something you've got to . . .

SCHERBAUM:
Hold it. If it weren't Max but just any old dog . . .

VERO LEWAND:
Oh, so that's it.

SCHERBAUM:

   Right.

VERO LEWAND:

   And what goes on out there, Flip, when they take
   the napalm and . . .
   [*She exits.* STARUSCH *enters.* SCHERBAUM *goes over
   to* STARUSCH]

SCHERBAUM:

   Good idea, getting a dog from the kennel.—I'll go
   to the kennel, and I'll buy a white spitz if they've
   got one.—Any idea what they ask for a spitz with
   no pedigree? [*Pause*] I'm always broke at the end
   of the month. [*Pause*] You can give it to me tomorrow.

STARUSCH [*begins to pace back and forth*]:

   Why do you debase your sacrifice?

SCHERBAUM:

   You're not supposed to ask questions. You're supposed to help.

STARUSCH:

   Yesterday everything had to be absolutely pure,
   and today you're ready to make a rotten compromise.

SCHERBAUM:

   The dog from the kennel was your idea.

STARUSCH:

   All right, you're afraid. But why should I and a
   nameless spitz, conceivably a bitch that has just
   been covered, pay for your cowardice?

SCHERBAUM:

   What if you had burned the spitz?

59

STARUSCH:

That would have been my free decision. Your plan is pure exploitation. Fine kind of heroism: Spare your own dog and sacrifice some nameless mutt. I don't like the way you add it up. [*Pause*]

SCHERBAUM:

Neither do I. You're probably right.
[*He runs off.* STARUSCH *puts on his coat, goes home by a roundabout way*]

STARUSCH:

I'm pleased with myself.—Am I pleased with myself?
[*He lets himself drop into his chair. The* DENTIST *enters.* STARUSCH *puts his hand on the telephone*]
What do you think, Doc?

DENTIST [*lifts the receiver*]:

You should have lent the boy the money. Time-consuming complications. The trip to the kennel. Selecting and buying a dog. Buying a leash. The presence of the spitz in his parents' apartment. Explaining to his mother, who's supposed to explain to his father—or vice versa. Then a friendship starts up between the dachshund and the spitz. Possibly your student has a little sister . . .

STARUSCH [*dully*]:

No. No sister.

DENTIST:

And this little sister likes the spitz and wants to keep it. The parents are in favor. All sorts of things could have messed up your student's plan any number of times. You should have lent the young man the money.

[*Hangs up, exits.* STARUSCH *jumps up, walks rapidly back to the school*]

STARUSCH [*running*]:

Scherbaum . . . [SCHERBAUM *enters*] You can have the money. A spitz without a pedigree costs between seventy and eighty marks.

SCHERBAUM [*smiling*]:

That was a momentary weakness, I want to apologize. It's Max or nothing. Or I might just as well burn a stuffed dog. Or several stuffed dogs. Vero Lewand has a whole zooful of them.

STARUSCH:

Too bad, Philipp. I wanted to help you.

SCHERBAUM:

I know you have my welfare at heart. [*He leaves* STARUSCH *standing and sits down at the school desk*] —Practically everybody has my welfare at heart.

[IRMGARD SEIFERT *enters, greets* STARUSCH]

IRMGARD SEIFERT [*next to the aquarium*]:

At least we agree that he's talented.

[VERO LEWAND *enters, sits down next to* SCHERBAUM *at the school desk*]

VERO LEWAND [*softly*]:

I'll show him. Flip, you wanta bet? I'll show him.

STARUSCH:

His father is an executive at Schering's.

61

IRMGARD SEIFERT:

In spite of better-than-average work in *your* subjects and in the realm of the Muses, it will be the same as last year, he'll barely slip through.

VERO LEWAND:

If he doesn't leave you alone, I'll go see him in his pad, Flip.

STARUSCH:

One can't speak of a conflict with his father. In one essay he wrote: My father, of course, was not a Nazi . . .

SCHERBAUM [*first reads, then acts out the essay*]:

My father was only an air-raid warden. An air-raid warden, of course, is not an anti-fascist. Frau Seifert is an anti-fascist. That's why we call her the Archangel. An air-raid warden is nothing. I am the son of an air-raid warden. Consequently I am the son of a nothing. My father is now a democrat, just as he was once an air-raid warden. He always does the right thing. Occasionally he says, "My generation made many mistakes"—he always says it in the right places. We never quarrel. Sometimes he says: "You too will have your experiences." And that too is correct because it's foreseeable that I'll have experiences. As a nothing or as an air-raid warden, which—as I have demonstrated—is the same thing. My mother often says: "You have a generous father." Sometimes she also says: "Your father is too generous." Then my generous nothing says: "Leave the boy be, Elisabeth, who knows what's in store for him." And that, too, is right. I like my father. He has such a sad way of looking out of the window. Then he always says: "You have it good in a peaceful world. I hope it stays that way. Our youth was different, quite different." I really do like my father. I like myself, too. I would've been a good air-raid warden. —And so on.

STARUSCH:
I had a hard time giving that essay a grade.

VERO LEWAND:
Take it from me, I'll show him good.
[*She and* SCHERBAUM *exit*]

IRMGARD SEIFERT:
For the grade, you could have substituted a comment on the highly derivative quality of the essay.
[*Both approach the couch by a roundabout way*]
Did you get home all right yesterday?

STARUSCH:
I indulged in two or three more beers and tried out a new combination: a coke with plain vodka.

IRMGARD SEIFERT [*sarcastically*]:
How frivolous, particularly since our relationship is distinguished by passionate moderation.

STARUSCH:
Perhaps we're afraid of destroying this rather passive condition by action.

IRMGARD SEIFERT:
Oh go on! There's nothing between us but our vocal cords.

STARUSCH:
Mightn't there also be a grain of unexpended sympathy?

IRMGARD SEIFERT:

Why do you keep bringing up irrelevant nonsense when I'm trying so hard to pursue a seventeen-year-old girl who did something, did something in my name, that I never . . .

STARUSCH:

That was more than twenty years ago. It falls under the statute of limitations.

IRMGARD SEIFERT:

What do years mean? Time can't turn such defeats into victories. [*Absently*] I'm tempted to agree with you but . . .

STARUSCH [*stands up, comes closer*]:

You've got to put that out of your mind once and for all.

IRMGARD SEIFERT:

. . . I can't help it . . . [STARUSCH *embraces her roughly and is about to shut her up by kissing her.* IRMGARD SEIFERT *frees herself and goes on talking unperturbed*] . . . because I'm more and more convinced that I must have been disappointed when nothing happened after my report. I am forced to assume I sent in another.

STARUSCH:

For God's sake! The farmer survived your first report as well as your purely imaginary second one.

IRMGARD SEIFERT:

That's not the question. You've got to realize . . .

STARUSCH:

You're alive. I came through too, by pure chance.

And my student, no, *our* Philipp Scherbaum is in
trouble . . .
[IRMGARD SEIFERT *jumps up.* STARUSCH *likewise*]

IRMGARD SEIFERT [*excitedly*]:
Will you stop talking about that school stuff? Nothing can exonerate me. These letters . . .
[STARUSCH *slaps her with his right hand. Pause,
and astonishment in both of them.* IRMGARD SEI-
FERT *looks for her cigarettes.* STARUSCH *hands her
one, and with the same hand that hit her he offers
her a light. While he slowly goes to his desk, the*
DENTIST *enters*]

DENTIST:
With one or both hands?

STARUSCH:
I cut off my colleague Irmgard Seifert's sentence
with a right-handed slap in the face.

DENTIST:
And now what? Tears?

STARUSCH:
She's smoking.

DENTIST:
To put it succinctly, your colleague is lonely.—
And how are you feeling?

STARUSCH:
A slap may be ridiculous, but it's still action.

DENTIST:
An intimate action, my dear friend. Such things
bring people together.
[*He exits.* STARUSCH *leaves the desk*]

IRMGARD SEIFERT:

You're right.

STARUSCH:

I'm sorry. I couldn't help it.

IRMGARD SEIFERT [*puts her cigarette out, sits down on the couch*]:

—You were saying something about Scherbaum.

STARUSCH:

It can happen any day now.

IRMGARD SEIFERT:

I agree with you that the boy is highly gifted.

STARUSCH:

Even Dr. Schüttlen says so. [*Parodies an elderly teacher*] In my subject, too, Scherbaum's above-average performance might be improved by greater concentration.

[*Both laugh artificially.* STARUSCH *sits down*]

IRMGARD SEIFERT:

Just six months ago Scherbaum showed me songs for the guitar that he had written himself. He sang them, too, at my request. You know the style— weltschmerz cum commitment. But definitely original. As we've said, he's highly gifted.

STARUSCH:

But he's stopped writing.

IRMGARD SEIFERT:

Then we must see to it that he starts writing again.

STARUSCH [*sarcastically*]:

Anti-napalm poetry to keep him from burning the dog?

IRMGARD SEIFERT [*coolly*]:

> May I remind you that you asked me to help you find a way out for young Scherbaum.

STARUSCH:

> I do appreciate it . . .
>
> [*Pause.* IRMGARD SEIFERT *jumps up abruptly, takes her coat*]

IRMGARD SEIFERT:

> Your slap only helped for a little while, Eberhard. I see myself sitting at an unvarnished wooden desk. I see myself writing in a neat hand a denunciation intended to cost a man his life.—By the way, I wore braids at the time.

BLACKOUT

scene seven

[IRMGARD SEIFERT *and* STARUSCH *walk up to* SCHERBAUM]

STARUSCH:

Say, Scherbaum, I haven't heard anything about your lyrical efforts in a long time. We think you ought to concentrate on songs, especially since you play the guitar . . .

SCHERBAUM:

Only lulls people to sleep.

IRMGARD SEIFERT:

You must know what power, what political power can be put into poetry.

SCHERBAUM:

You don't mean it.

IRMGARD SEIFERT [*calmly*]:

Think of Tucholsky, think of Brecht. We have had a tradition of political songs since Wedekind.

SCHERBAUM:

They don't start anything moving. With luck, you can make money: They're soul massage. Ask Vero. [*Calls*] Vero! [*She joins them*] Isn't that right? When I sang you my most militant song—my "Beggar's Song" with the revolutionary theme "Bread for the World"—you just bawled and said: Cool. Really cool.

VERO LEWAND:

You just can't stand it when somebody likes something.

SCHERBAUM:

Because to you it's only a passing mood.

VERO LEWAND:

What makes you so sure about that?

SCHERBAUM [*to* STARUSCH]:

To her, it's all a matter of feeling. [*To* VERO LEWAND] Now listen: What I wanted to say in my song is that charity only increases misery, that it only benefits the givers, the haves, the oppressors.

VERO LEWAND:

That's exactly what I dug. And a year ago, when you wrote "Picking Stars," I got going right away with a hacksaw in Dahlem and those places where the Mercedes are parked all over . . . [*Trills*]: Picking stars, picking stars . . .

SCHERBAUM:

Oh, stop it.

STARUSCH:

Your discussion proves to me at least that an activist song still has the power to start a debate.

SCHERBAUM:

A few big tears, followed by star-picking.

STARUSCH:

All right, Scherbaum. You don't believe in words. You want action. A public act. Let's suppose you carry out your plan. They'll beat you up. If they don't kill you, at least they'll send you to the hospital. That's what you want, isn't it—the reaction of the public? Headlines in the morning paper. Prosecution by the SPCA. In spite of votes to the contrary, you'll be expelled from school. And a week later not a soul will be talking about it, because something else will be making headlines, maybe a two-headed calf.—Instead you sit down and write "The Ballad of Max, the Dachs."

SCHERBAUM:

Then what?

STARUSCH:

If your song is good, it will live, a lot longer than any headlines.

VERO LEWAND:

Just what I was waiting for. He wants you to write for eternity. Just like a schoolteacher. The man's a paper tiger.

STARUSCH [*laughs*]:

Right you are. And your paper tiger even admits that poems seldom produce an immediate effect, that the effect comes slowly and often too late.

VERO LEWAND:

But we want to be effective now, this minute.

STARUSCH:

You want headlines that will be displaced by headlines.

VERO LEWAND:

I don't know what will happen tomorrow.

IRMGARD SEIFERT:

That's cheap, Veronika, and not worthy of you.

SCHERBAUM:

I don't even know what *is* worthy.

IRMGARD SEIFERT:

You in particular should try to understand the world with all its variety and inconsistencies . . .

SCHERBAUM [*agitated and softly*]:

I don't want to understand. Do you understand? I know, I know, everything can be explained. How does it go? Because the vital interests of the United States are affected.

STARUSCH:

Exactly. Unfortunately. When ten years ago the revolt in Budapest affected the vital interests of the Soviet Union, they ruthlessly . . .

SCHERBAUM:

I know that! I know about it! Everything can be explained. Everything can be understood. If this . . . then that. On the one hand it's bad, but on the other hand to prevent worse. Peace has its price. Our freedom isn't for free. If we give in today, it will be our turn tomorrow. I've read that napalm obviates the need for nuclear weapons. The localization of war is a triumph of reason. My father says: If it weren't for the atom bomb, we'd have had the Third World War long ago . . . He's right. It can be proved. We ought to be grateful, and keep the little conflict boiling, so that no larger . . . And write poems that won't be effective until the day after tomorrow.—No. Nothing will be changed. People burn slowly every day. I'll do it. A dog, that'll get 'em. [*Pause*]

VERO LEWAND [*softly and enthusiastically*]:

Cool, the way you say that.
[SCHERBAUM's *left hand jerks up,* STARUSCH *prevents the slap*]

71

STARUSCH:

Considering the intransigence of your attitude, I'd
advise you to avoid acts of violence, Scherbaum.
—Anyway, recess is over.
[SCHERBAUM *and* VERO LEWAND *exit. He puts his
arm around her shoulder*]

STARUSCH [*to* IRMGARD SEIFERT]:

Unlike me, he's left-handed.—They'd stomp him to
pieces, Doc, with stiletto heels.
[*The* DENTIST *enters*]

DENTIST:

And the T.V. people will focus their camera on it
and ask for working space: "Be reasonable. Step
back just a tiny bit. How can we be expected to report objectively, if you prevent us from . . ."

IRMGARD SEIFERT [*next to the aquarium*]:

Believe me, Eberhard: You could crucify Christ on
the Avenue today in the rush hour and raise the
cross. The people will just watch—and take pictures, if they've got their cameras.

STARUSCH:

But when they see a dog . . .

DENTIST:

We can assume that your student knows what's in
store for him in view of the intense animal cult of
this city's populace.

IRMGARD SEIFERT:

You really ought to pull yourself together and put
an end to this nonsense.

STARUSCH:

You mean turn in a report?

DENTIST:

Well, you might be concerned about your position as a teacher.

STARUSCH:

But what can I . . . Write a letter to my senator on the Education Committee? My dear Mr. Evers . . . One of my students has decided . . . My dear Senator, in June of last year you stated at a meeting: "May we have the moral courage of Adolf Diesterweg!" I therefore beg you to join me in accompanying my student on his hard road in order that your presence may lend the public burning of a dog the pedagogical significance to which we all aspire . . . [*Pause*] Yours respectfully . . . For heaven's sake, Doc, what should I do? Dammit all. Help me, please!

DENTIST [*pause*]:

Ask your student to inspect the intended scene of action with you. Maybe something will come of it. Call again at noon. My practice never lets up. The world could stop, and still people would come here with their mouths full of lamentation. [*He exits*]

IRMGARD SEIFERT:

Don't you think, Eberhard, that it's awfully quiet in the midst of noise? We ought to do something. Do something, do anything. [*She exits*]

STARUSCH:

Do something. Do something. Anything. Do something. Shall I rehearse? Talk to the mirror while I'm shaving, till it fogs up: What else can I say, Philipp?

[SCHERBAUM *enters, sits down behind the school desk.* STARUSCH *remains at a distance*]

SCHERBAUM:
You've got to help. Or I won't be able to do it.

STARUSCH:
Even if you're right, it's not worth it.

SCHERBAUM:
If you encourage me, I think . . .

STARUSCH:
I was the same. We were against everybody and everything. It was wartime.

SCHERBAUM:
It's always wartime.

STARUSCH:
I didn't want anything explained to me. Just like you.

SCHERBAUM:
And now?

STARUSCH:
I didn't want to turn into what I am now.—But even if I am, as you see, what I am—just as I saw others for what they were—I nevertheless know I have turned into something I didn't want to be—and that you wouldn't want to be. If I were like you, I'd have to say: Do it! [*More softly*] Do it.

SCHERBAUM:
But you're not saying anything.

STARUSCH:
Why don't I say: Let him burn?

74

SCHERBAUM [*quietly*]:

Because you're jealous, you'd like to do it yourself, but you can't. Because you're a has-been. Because you're not afraid. Because it's all the same to you whether you do it or not. Because you've been through everything. Because you have your teeth fixed for later. Because you figure out the consequences before you act, so that the consequences will fall in with your calculations. Because you don't like yourself. Because you're rational, which doesn't prevent you from being stupid.

STARUSCH:

All right, Philipp. Do it. But it won't accomplish anything. It'll become a memory for you, enormous. You'll never get over it. Forever after you'll have to say: When I was seventeen, I. When I was seventeen, I was an activist.

[SCHERBAUM *gets up.* STARUSCH *takes his coat and goes over to* SCHERBAUM] If you feel like it, Scherbaum, we can go take a look at the place together, so you can see what you're letting yourself in for.

SCHERBAUM:

All right. But don't get your hopes up.—I won't chicken out.

BLACKOUT

[STARUSCH *is standing at his desk.* IRMGARD SEI-FERT *is sitting on the couch. The* DENTIST *is work-ing at his lab table. In the background* SCHERBAUM *and* VERO LEWAND *are standing with their bicycles*]

VERO LEWAND:

What does it have to do with Old Hardy?

SCHERBAUM:

He insisted on coming along: to inspect the scene of action.

IRMGARD SEIFERT:

Well, Eberhard, was your experiment worthwhile?

STARUSCH:

We agreed to meet without the dog, but Scherbaum brought the dachshund.

SCHERBAUM:

Max came along. I wanted to get him used to it.

STARUSCH:

The restaurant terrace was packed: the usual stately ladies.

SCHERBAUM:

Old Hardy made jokes, as usual.

VERO LEWAND:

That's him all over.

STARUSCH:

If we proceed on the assumption that a jelly dough-
nut contains two hundred calories, it becomes su-
perfluous to ask how many calories are contained
in a piece of Black Forest cherry cake with whipped
cream.

[SCHERBAUM *moves away from* VERO LEWAND, STA-
RUSCH *from his desk. Both front stage*]

SCHERBAUM:

There they sit.

STARUSCH:

They're stuffing because they're worried.

SCHERBAUM:

They paste everything over with cake.

STARUSCH:

As long as they eat cake, they're happy and probably
not dangerous.

[*Both stare*]

SCHERBAUM:

It's got to stop.

STARUSCH:

Actually it's just funny.

SCHERBAUM:

Those are the grown-ups. That's what they wanted
and now they've got it. Freedom of choice and second helpings, that's what they mean by democracy.

[STARUSCH *to the desk.* SCHERBAUM *remains on the
apron*]

STARUSCH [*to* IRMGARD SEIFERT]:

I conceded that his far-fetched comparison had its

77

points, and I tried to cheer him up with jokes about too much jewelry. [*To* SCHERBAUM] Just imagine those overloaded ladies sitting there naked.

SCHERBAUM:

They won't shovel in any more cake. The image of Max, burning and writhing, will stand in their way.

VERO LEWAND:

I don't get it. Why doesn't he do it? That would be practice. A departure from theory. A concrete reality, Flip. Do it!

IRMGARD SEIFERT [*to* STARUSCH]:

You should have called Scherbaum's attention— not once but many times—to the danger of physical violence.

STARUSCH:

Right here, where you're standing, Scherbaum, they'll beat you to a pulp.

IRMGARD SEIFERT:

And the passers-by—you should have said—will form a circle and will argue about whether that lump of humanity on the sidewalk burned a schnauzer, a terrier, a dachshund, or a pekinese.

SCHERBAUM:

They'll toss their cookies.

VERO LEWAND:

So do it, Flip. Do it.

STARUSCH:

Most of the ladies will call for their checks. But other ladies in similar furs and similar hats will move in . . .

VERO LEWAND:
   Do it, Flip, do it!

STARUSCH:
   They'll point their dessert forks; they'll show each
   other where it happened. Right here, Scherbaum.
   Right here where we're standing.

VERO LEWAND:
   And you listened to that? You just listened?

STARUSCH:
   They'll say the whole thing is barbarous, especially
   because your Max won't burn quietly, patiently, and
   quickly. I can see him jumping and writhing. I can
   hear him whimpering, Philipp.

IRMGARD SEIFERT:
   Could you tell me, dear colleague, what purpose
   this excursion was supposed to serve for you and
   your student?

STARUSCH:
   Scherbaum vomited violently and heaved several
   times onto the sidewalk.

SCHERBAUM:
   I puked.

VERO LEWAND:
   Right onto the sidewalk?

SCHERBAUM:
   They didn't. I did.

STARUSCH:
   The mechanism of a few dessert forks stalled.

VERO LEWAND [*softly*]:
   Cool, Flip.

SCHERBAUM:

I threw up, I tell you, I really threw up.

VERO LEWAND:

And Max?

SCHERBAUM:

He whimpered, what else?

STARUSCH:

Before a circle could form—the pedestrian traffic had already come to a halt—I pulled Philipp and the whimpering dachshund into the next street. [*He goes up to* SCHERBAUM]

SCHERBAUM:

What a flop.

STARUSCH:

That was more effective, Philipp, than if you had burned the dog.

SCHERBAUM:

But they don't even know why I . . .

STARUSCH:

The look on their faces! I tell you, Philipp, the look on their faces . . .
[SCHERBAUM *leaves* STARUSCH *standing and goes back to* VERO LEWAND]

SCHERBAUM:

Now you know what kind of goof I am.

VERO LEWAND:

It was just a rehearsal.

SCHERBAUM:

I'm not supposed to . . . *they* are.

VERO LEWAND:

They will, too. For sure, Flip. They will, too.

SCHERBAUM:

I'm a failure.

VERO LEWAND:

Oh go on, man. You've just got to do it.
[*Both exit*]

IRMGARD SEIFERT [*stands up*]:

Well, all in all. You were successful. [*Sarcastically, as she exits*] But that probably wasn't a genuine solution, either.

STARUSCH:

That whipped cream, those tons of crisp pastries, those abundantly available sweets, that flood of creamy chocolate, all this consumption is to blame. Yes, Doc. They've ceased to be human beings, they're just consumers.

DENTIST [*laughs*]:

If you set your mind to it, you can see even Black Forest cherry cake as a symbol of evil. Your generalizations are unsound. Our society, even when it crowds onto café terraces, is rather more complex.

STARUSCH:

That's my dentist: tolerant.

DENTIST:

There's no point in concocting a bogeyman out of rich cake, fancy hats, and worry blubber, especially as it won't help your student for you to adopt his narrow outlook.

STARUSCH:

He's married. Has three children. Practices a profession that gets results. That makes it easy for him to be tolerant.

DENTIST:

My mother, for instance, a sensible Prussian lady, but not without humor and savoir faire, got into the habit of visiting the Kempinski Café terrace twice a month, after shopping. She ate a single piece of cake—honey nutroll—without whipped cream. A relatively minor sin, even you will admit.

STARUSCH:

You can talk, Doc. You see human beings as vulnerable, imperfect contraptions requiring care. But anyone who wants more, who demands that man should surpass himself, gain awareness of his exploited state, and prepare for a change in established conditions; anyone who, like my student, sees around him nothing but replete dullness, will perceive the mechanical consumption of cake as the very clockwork of capitalist society.

DENTIST:

I admit that his relatively closed consumer society must appear sinister to a boy of seventeen, because he can't understand it. But you, an experienced pedagogue, you ought to be on your guard against seeing a supposed, or even an actual, opponent as the devil incarnate.

STARUSCH:

I have a fair right to be unfair!

DENTIST:

That's a doubtful privilege.

STARUSCH:

And what about your appeasements?

DENTIST:

An attempt to differentiate.

STARUSCH [*dropping onto the couch*]:

He relativizes everything.

DENTIST:

If I, as a dentist, were to say such things . . .

STARUSCH:

Wise guy. Mr. Objectivity. Efficient professional monomaniac.

DENTIST:

After all, every day I have to fight tooth decay caused or promoted by excessive pastry consumption and sweets as such.

STARUSCH:

Affable technocrat. Enlightened philistine.

DENTIST:

All the same, I refuse to advocate the abolition of pastry and hard candy.

STARUSCH:

Reactionary modernist. Social welfare quack.

DENTIST:

I can only counsel moderation and—when it's not too late—repair the damage.

STARUSCH:

Tooth-plumber. Tooth-plumber!

DENTIST:

I must caution you against generalizations which on the one hand simulate great leaps forward but on the other hand in the final analysis make for total paralysis.

STARUSCH [*jumps up*]:

On the one hand—on the other hand. But what am I going to do?

DENTIST:

Let me make a suggestion: Bring the young man to see me. I'd like to meet him.

BLACKOUT

[STARUSCH *and* SCHERBAUM *are sitting on two chairs near the dentist's chair. Between them a small table with illustrated magazines.* SCHERBAUM *is leafing through them.* VERO LEWAND *is standing center with her bicycle*]

VERO LEWAND:
Now he's dragged you off again, and you let him.

SCHERBAUM [*without looking up*]:
If it makes him happy. What a guy won't do for his teacher.

VERO LEWAND:
But when I say come on, we're going to discuss base and superstructure, you talk your way out of it with shorthand.

SCHERBAUM:
My base—stenography.

VERO LEWAND:
Our group thinks you're slipping into the petit bourgeois perspective.

SCHERBAUM:
And you smell of the group. Group smog.

VERO LEWAND:
You never have time for me.

SCHERBAUM:

You know what I'm planning.

VERO LEWAND:

Do it, Flip. If you don't do it, I'll do something. And I'm not just talking, I really will.

SCHERBAUM [*looking up*]:

What?

VERO LEWAND:

I'll do it. For sure, Flip, I'll do it.
[*Rides off on her bike.* SCHERBAUM *leafs on. The* DENTIST *enters*]

DENTIST:

Won't you come in? To tell the truth, I was expecting your student.

STARUSCH:

Here he is. But don't expect too much of him.

DENTIST [*inviting* STARUSCH *with a gesture to take a seat in the dentist's chair*]:

And please, keep you tongue way down—nice and relaxed. [*While he shines the light into* STARUSCH's *oral cavity, aside to* SCHERBAUM] I've heard about your unusual project. Even though it would be impossible for me to do such a thing, I'll try to understand you. If you have to do it—but only if you really have to—then do it. [*To* STARUSCH] Well, that looks a lot better. The inflammation has subsided. But maybe we'll extend the rest period just a little. [*To* SCHERBAUM] This, by the way, is my semi-automatic Ritter chair. This is the adjustable instrument table—moves at the touch of a button. The instruments are not visible to the patient, but I'll show them to you: the elevator. The molar forceps. Here my fully automatic air-drill. Velocity 350,000 revolutions a minute. Works soundlessly without vibration. [*To* STARUSCH] These high-speed drills require an extremely steady hand. An eighth of a second's inattention and the pulp is roasted. [*To* SCHERBAUM] And here a collection of porcelain bridges ready to be mounted. You see, there are always people who lack indispensable teeth.

SCHERBAUM [*points to several graphs hanging on the wall*]:
What's that there? Looks exciting.

DENTIST:
Exciting and alarming. Those are caries curves. As you may know, caries is to be found all over the world, a by-product of civilization. However, modern dental science—in contrast to politics—can point to achievements which show conclusively that progress is possible if we confine ourselves strictly to the findings of natural science. Any speculation beyond that leads necessarily to ideological mystification or—as we should say—to erroneous diagnosis.

SCHERBAUM:
You're right. Just what I've been thinking. That's why I want to burn my dog in public. [*Pause*]

DENTIST:
By the way, as you were talking I believe I noticed that your front teeth . . . Did you bite your lips as a child? Like this: with your upper front teeth over your lower lip. You have a distal bite. If you don't mind.
[*He urges* SCHERBAUM *into the dentist's chair.*

STARUSCH *leaves the chair;* SCHERBAUM *seats himself*]

SCHERBAUM:
Is it expensive?

DENTIST [*smiling*]:
Free treatments are sometimes given to fellow devotees of science.

SCHERBAUM:
But don't hurt me.

DENTIST:
Hurting—is not my profession.
[*While the* DENTIST *examines* SCHERBAUM, STARUSCH *withdraws to center stage.* VERO LEWAND *enters*]

STARUSCH:
Ever since the 6th of February, 1967, I see Scherbaum in the dentist's chair.

VERO LEWAND:
Has Flip let you manipulate him again?

STARUSCH:
He has taken a seat in the dentist's chair—if that's what you mean by manipulation.

VERO LEWAND:
I'm warning you, Old Hardy.

STARUSCH:
He did it of his own free will.

VERO LEWAND:
If you don't stop demoralizing Flip, I'll demoralize you.

STARUSCH [*smiling*]:

Nothing is easier than demoralizing a liberal teacher.

VERO LEWAND:

And I once thought you were left-wing, one of us. But all you want to do is interpret—when it comes to changing it, you're not there. [*She exits*]

STARUSCH:

She's right. I'm not there. [*Back to the* DENTIST]

DENTIST:

You should have come to me with your milk teeth.

SCHERBAUM:

Is it bad?

DENTIST:

We'll make a set of x-rays. Then we'll see. [*He x-rays* SCHERBAUM'*s lower and upper jaws, taking notes*] The four lower incisors.—Well? Did that hurt?

SCHERBAUM [*leaves the dentist's chair*]:

By the way, I think that stuff about caries is very interesting. And thanks a lot.
[*He exits.* STARUSCH *walks slowly to his desk*]

STARUSCH:

Splendid, Doc. You've succeeded in providing my student with a scientific rationalization for his irrational plan.

DENTIST:

He has a distal bite. But with a little patience, treatment is still possible even at his age.

STARUSCH:

You encouraged him. Encouraged him!—I'm going to sit down this minute and draft an affidavit for the use of the lawyer who will defend my student. [*At the desk*]

DENTIST:

You could start by minimizing the whole thing. Call it student shenanigans.

STARUSCH:

I will erect a hedge of literary comparisons around Scherbaum's act. I'll cite surrealist and futurist manfestoes. Aragon and Marinetti are my witnesses. The happening as an art form. The Dadaists . . .

DENTIST:

Black humor. Better steer clear of it. In this country wit is fed by feeling and occasionally by malice. —But how about an assist from the classics?— You could cast your student in the role of Tasso and sway the court with the worldly wisdom of Antonio.

STARUSCH [*writing*]:

Just as the worldly-wise Antonio countered the poetic excesses of young Tasso with sober perspicacity, so may the court arrive at a magnanimous decision in the spirit of the poet Goethe. [*He quotes*] "Thus in the end the boatman clings / Fast to the rock that was to be his doom."

DENTIST:

Wind up on a note of liberalism. That shouldn't be hard for you.

STARUSCH:

A nation which looks upon the activated confusion

of so highly gifted and hypersensitive a student as a public danger demonstrates its insecurity and attempts to replace the benefits of democratic indulgence by authoritarian harshness.

DENTIST:
Excellent. That's the ticket.

STARUSCH [*stands up, dons his coat*]:
In the end all that's left of the fish is the bones. The man who had carloads of solutions to offer now serenades emptiness until it becomes fashionable: a coat of skimpy cut lacking sleeves, buttons, and pockets. Only the cloth remains. Nobody takes the blame. What do we play next?

BLACKOUT

IRMGARD SEIFERT:

Well, Eberhard?

STARUSCH:

First he sat down in the dentist's chair to see what it was like.

IRMGARD SEIFERT:

Your pedagogical solicitude seems to be unbounded —and not just for me.

STARUSCH:

I've had enough. I'm only a teacher. I don't want to dig deeper. Do you understand? I want it to stop.

IRMGARD SEIFERT:

It won't stop, Eberhard.

STARUSCH [*sharply*]:

I know.—Yesterday I went to a party . . . [*Stands up*]

IRMGARD SEIFERT:

That early imprinting or—as you call it—my thing in the Harz . . .

STARUSCH [*sharply*]:

I said: Yesterday I went to a party.

IRMGARD SEIFERT:

I denounced him.—Was it fun?

[VERO LEWAND, SCHERBAUM, *the* DENTIST *enter*]

. . .

VERO LEWAND:

They're way on the left politically. They're our people.

STARUSCH:

Scherbaum and his girl friend talked me into . . .

VERO LEWAND:

The one with the Castro lid is our farthest left underground publisher.

IRMGARD SEIFERT:

You really ought to keep your distance from . . .

VERO LEWAND:

And he's just come from Milan where he met people who'd just come from Bolivia where they talked with Ché.

STARUSCH:

Sixty people were crowded into the rent-controlled, practically furnitureless apartment, minus seven who were just leaving, plus eleven who were just arriving or trying to arrive.—What are they talking about?

VERO LEWAND:

Themselves, of course.

IRMGARD SEIFERT:

With little Lewand's help you must have found a bit of standing room.

STARUSCH:

And what do they want?

VERO LEWAND:

Oh, change. To change the world.

STARUSCH:

> We both stood there alienated, Scherbaum as well as myself. One couldn't help noticing the extravagant uniformity of dress and the sweeping gestures that seemed to be banking on a hidden camera . . .

VERO LEWAND:

> Ho! Ho! Ho Chi Minh! [*She underlines the revolutionary yell with rhythmic clapping. Later the yells and clapping subside somewhat*]

STARUSCH [*moves away from both*]:

> Scherbaum became so quiet that I was afraid somebody would notice. I myself . . .

IRMGARD SEIFERT:

> Too old. You're too old. And maybe you were a little envious that the young people could be so bouncy and left-wing.

STARUSCH:

> I said to myself: Get with it!

IRMGARD SEIFERT:

> But you weren't the only defoliated specimen in his late thirties. [*She claps the revolutionary rhythm suggestively*]

STARUSCH:

> They all joined in and yelled themselves back into their cracked-voice adolescence.
>
> [VERO LEWAND *grabs him and pulls him to center stage*]

VERO LEWAND:

> Why don't you get with it, Old Hardy?

STARUSCH:

> I never get with it.

VERO LEWAND [*rotating around him*]:
> No, all you can do is break it up. Demoralize. Turn people off. Interpret everything and change nothing. Careerist! Reformist! Typical drubber! Social fascist!
> [*She claps the rhythm again.* STARUSCH *returns to the desk*]

STARUSCH:
> It seemed to me that Scherbaum was beginning to age wordlessly at my side.
> [VERO LEWAND *pushes* SCHERBAUM *to the center*]

VERO LEWAND:
> This is my friend Flip.

STARUSCH:
> Two girls accosted Scherbaum: Is this him, Vero? Are you the Scherbaum everybody's talking about?

VERO LEWAND:
> Right outside the restaurant, I tell you. With real gasoline. Poof! No, in the daytime, in the afternoon. Tell 'em, Flip. They admire you, honest.

SCHERBAUM:
> Teeny bopper!

VERO LEWAND:
> Flip, please . . .

SCHERBAUM:
> Let's get out of here. This stinks.
> [*He pulls* VERO LEWAND *with him. Both exit*]

IRMGARD SEIFERT:
> Oh, well, the usual kid stuff!
> [IRMGARD SEIFERT *exits.* STARUSCH *to the center*]

95

. . .

STARUSCH:

He started slapping her on the staircase and continued in the yard . . .

[SCHERBAUM *and* VERO LEWAND *enter. He keeps slapping her, slapping her hard*]

VERO LEWAND:

Flip. No. Please. Flip.

STARUSCH [*separates them*]:

That'll do. Let's drink a peaceable beer. [*He gives* VERO LEWAND *his handkerchief*]

VERO LEWAND:

Don't send me home now, Flip. Please.

[*All three are at the bar.* VERO LEWAND *tilts her head back; her nose is bleeding*]

STARUSCH:

Suppose we make up.

SCHERBAUM:

What else?

STARUSCH:

How did you like my dentist?

SCHERBAUM:

He knows what he wants.

STARUSCH:

He's got to, in his job.

SCHERBAUM:

I didn't know all that stuff about caries. And how early it starts.

STARUSCH:

And your distal bite? Will you get it fixed?

SCHERBAUM:
> When this thing is over with.

STARUSCH:
> Still going through with it?

SCHERBAUM:
> She can't stop me. Or did you expect me to back out because a couple of teeny boppers who think they're leftists say cool, really cool.

STARUSCH:
> That's not fair, Philipp. Vero . . .

SCHERBAUM [*sharply*]:
> Her? She reads her Mao the way my mother laps up Rilke. With her feelings and nothing else. [*To* VERO] Admit that you read without thinking.

VERO LEWAND:
> Flip, please. I thought . . .

SCHERBAUM:
> Come on, stop it. It's finished.
> [*He puts his arm around her shoulder and exits with her.* STARUSCH *slowly moves to the desk*]

STARUSCH [*while* SCHERBAUM *and* VERO LEWAND *are exiting, then on his way*]:
> Make up again.—The internal conflicts of the left are not a pretty sight.—You just don't know how far to the right you'll find yourselves one of these days. My dentist, for instance, where does he stand? [*At the desk, puts his hand on the telephone*] Well, Doc? Go on, say something.
> [*The* DENTIST *enters*]
> . . .

DENTIST [*laughing*]:

I'm a radical proponent of prophylaxis.—By the way, your student has already called.

STARUSCH:

Does that mean Scherbaum is interested in the state of his teeth?

DENTIST:

Who isn't?

STARUSCH:

Well?

DENTIST:

First, he asked if he shouldn't apply at the school health service . . .

STARUSCH:

How sensible.

DENTIST:

That's up to you, I said. Of course, I can arrange an appointment for you at any time.

STARUSCH:

Did he respond?

DENTIST:

I didn't want to press him.

STARUSCH:

And not a word about the dog?

DENTIST:

He didn't mention him directly. But he thanked me for reinforcing his determination. Your student ought to have more encouragement. We ought to encourage him. Understand? Encourage him constantly.

[*The* DENTIST *exits.* STARUSCH *sits down*]

STARUSCH:

He's experimenting with pedagogy. Shall I change horses and become a dentist?—One way or the other: I'm losing touch with Scherbaum.—Hoho-Ho . . . I can't do it . . . [*He claps his hands and tries the revolutionary rhythm*] 225987

BLACKOUT

scene eleven

IRMGARD SEIFERT:

I have to admit, I'm beginning to understand Scherbaum better. It is the boy's mission to accomplish what we—I, and you, too—were not able to accomplish. If only I could encourage him.

[SCHERBAUM *and* VERO LEWAND *enter with their bicycles. The* DENTIST *takes a seat at his lab table.* STARUSCH *in the vicinity of the desk.* IRMGARD SEIFERT *goes up to* SCHERBAUM]

VERO LEWAND:

Watch out, Flip. The Archangel is homing in on you.

IRMGARD SEIFERT:

You're right, Philipp. What good are our substitute solutions to you, the daily capitulations of adults.

STARUSCH:

My colleague is taking your advice and trying to encourage Scherbaum.

IRMGARD SEIFERT:

We have lost our capacity for spontaneous action.

STARUSCH:

You're included in the "we."

IRMGARD SEIFERT:

How often I have determined to step up before the

class and bear witness: That's how *I* was, when *I* was seventeen. That's what I did when I was seventeen.—Help me, Philipp. Lead us, lead me, lest our failure become universal.

DENTIST:

Well? Is she encouraging him?

VERO , LEWAND:

We're just not interested in what you did when you were seventeen. It's probably true that you did or didn't do something when you were seventeen. Everybody did something at seventeen. Old Hardy more than anybody. Whenever we tell him what's going on in Vietnam, he talks about his days in a teen-age gang when the war was on and makes speeches about early anarchism. We don't want teen-age gangs. Flip's no anarchist, not even slightly. What you're saying is pure subjectivism. [*To* SCHERBAUM] Come on, let's go. Or the Archangel will put on the old record again.
[*Both park their bicycles, laughing, sit down at the school table*]

IRMGARD SEIFERT:

But there must be an ear to listen . . . Always this lightfooted language. If I could only stutter. And not keep a teacher's distance. Or could believe in something or other. Like a Catholic's piece of painted plaster. Something for the day after tomorrow. But even socialism. Even my aquarium, this attempt to establish peace in a limited sphere. Eating their own brood. Disgusting. I retch. But nothing comes up.
[STARUSCH *walks up to* IRMGARD SEIFERT]
. . .

STARUSCH:

Well, have you encouraged Scherbaum?

IRMGARD SEIFERT [*pulling herself together*]:

He sees only his deed and not the shadow it will cast: its exemplary, redemptive quality. [*She exits*]

STARUSCH:

Even if Scherbaum doesn't do anything, he's raked up our mud.

DENTIST [*stands up*]:

Your colleague's capacity for enthusiasm will give your student a notion of the followers who will sprout up around him after his act. She's building him a monument. Even before the deed is done the hero worship is starting in. [*Laughs and exits*]

STARUSCH:

No, Doc. He's not like that, not a hero. Not interested in leading or gaining supporters. He hasn't got the fanatical stare. He's not even rude. He was never pushy. He doesn't want to be editor-in-chief. His voice doesn't proclaim. He's no messiah. He brings no message. He's entirely different. [*He goes to the school desk, mildly lecturing*] What even Marx realized relatively late, that a revolution can be carried out only with the help of a revolutionary class that has nothing to lose and everything to gain, ought to be familiar knowledge to us today. We certainly shouldn't try to provoke misinterpretations.—Scherbaum, you have seen how eager my colleague, Frau Seifert, is to misunderstand you.

VERO LEWAND:

Flip can't select his followers.

STARUSCH:

All the same, I must warn you not to promote a pseudo-revolutionary hysteria.

SCHERBAUM:

I don't know if you know anything about theoretical mathematics . . . I've developed a formula . . .

VERO LEWAND [*jumps up, in motion*]:

And it's right. The lower house meets on Thursday. Flip will be more or less recovered by Friday; he'll announce a press conference in the hospital and make a statement. Messages of solidarity will start pouring in. Not only here: all over Germany. Dogs will be burned in several big cities. Later foreign countries will join in. That's called the ritualized form of provocation.

SCHERBAUM:

I'll show you the formula.

VERO LEWAND:

Later, Flip, when the thing has come off.
[*She sits down again. The* DENTIST *enters*]

STARUSCH:

What if it doesn't work? If they kill him?

DENTIST [*laughing*]:

Then the formula was wrong.

STARUSCH:

If the clear weather holds until next Wednesday, you won't get a chance to correct Scherbaum's distal bite.

DENTIST:

If he acts.—Tell me, my friend, aside from the

103

exemplary influences which you as a teacher transmit, does your student have an ideal? You know, we always orient ourselves by guiding stars.
[*He exits.* IRMGARD SEIFERT *enters*]

IRMGARD SEIFERT:

The men of the 20th of July? Stauffenberg, for instance.

STARUSCH:

In your case, that South American revolutionary Ché Guevara ought to . . .

SCHERBAUM [*laughs*]:

He's Vero's type. She needs a pin-up.

VERO LEWAND:

What about you? Who did you pin up on your wall?
[*Pause.* SCHERBAUM *gets up, goes to the blackboard and writes the name Helmut Hübener*]

SCHERBAUM:

Nobody ever heard of him. Not mentioned in school lectures. Belonged to a sect. Something like the Mormons. Came from Hamburg. But they had their stuff printed in Kiel. A group of four. Apprentices and clerks. He was executed in Plötzensee, Berlin, on October 27, 1942. Tortured beforehand, of course. He was seventeen. Distributed leaflets for more than a year. Started when he was just sixteen. You see, he could take shorthand and even knew Morse code.—I'm taking a course in stenography myself. When I've finished this thing with Max, I'm going to study radio communications and telegraphy.
[*Both exit*]
.   .   .

STARUSCH:

Shorthand and Morse code. I don't know either.

IRMGARD SEIFERT [*over to* STARUSCH]:

I feel a little sorry for you. Didn't you hope that Scherbaum would take you as his ideal?

STARUSCH:

Maybe I did know Morse code when I was seventeen.—Seventeen-year-olds often know things they can hardly remember, or don't care to, when they're forty.—Isn't that so, my dear colleague?

IRMGARD SEIFERT:

Thanks for the reminder.
[*She exits.* SCHERBAUM *enters, but keeps his distance*]

SCHERBAUM:

How old was Kiesinger when Helmut Hübener was executed?

STARUSCH:

We can figure it out: He joined the Party in thirty-three. He was twenty-nine at the time.

SCHERBAUM:

And now he's Chancellor. Has been for two months.

STARUSCH:

Nobody raised any objections.

SCHERBAUM [*softly*]:

I can't stand it. When I see him . . .

STARUSCH:

Maybe he's come to realize . . .

SCHERBAUM [*agitated, but not loud*]:

Him, of all people, him . . . And now they let him

. . . I mean, now he can . . . I mean, now again
he can . . . I'll do it, Doc! [*Loudly*] I'll do it. You've
got injections, Doc. I mean, against pain. There
must be some. That work on a dog, so he won't. I
mean. Or maybe you know a vet, who . . . Or
maybe you get the stuff without prescription, Doc,
in the drugstore.

[*He runs off. The* DENTIST *enters*]

DENTIST [*sharply, confused*]:
Did you put him up to it?

STARUSCH [*sarcastically*]:
I presume you didn't refuse the youngster the small
favor.

DENTIST:
Naturally I had to say no.

STARUSCH:
Didn't you want to encourage him, give him con-
stant encouragement?

DENTIST:
That's going too far. Where will that get us? If,
if . . . [*Loudly and excitedly*] My solicitude has its
limits! You understand?

STARUSCH [*softly*]:
Scherbaum alone.—I wonder if he's grinding away
at shorthand now?

DENTIST:
The young man seemed desperate. He has a slight
lisp.

[SCHERBAUM *enters*]

. . .

SCHERBAUM:

I understand, Doc. As a doctor you've got to act like a doctor. No matter what. [*He exits*]

DENTIST:

Really, an astonishing young man . . . and exemplary.

BLACKOUT

scene twelve

[*The* DENTIST *in his place.* STARUSCH *at his desk.*
IRMGARD SEIFERT *in front of the couch.* SCHERBAUM
at the school table. VERO LEWAND *is standing center.*
She is wearing a duffel coat and is applying
make-up clumsily]

IRMGARD SEIFERT:
A student has made insinuations. I refused to listen,
but I still must ask you to explain to me how that
silly goose . . .

VERO LEWAND:
I'll do it.

SCHERBAUM:
You'd better stay out of this, I say.

IRMGARD SEIFERT:
I'm waiting. [*Sits down*]

STARUSCH:
I give up.

DENTIST:
A luxury that I can't afford. [*Exits*]

STARUSCH:
What kind of move do we accomplish? Changes in
the daily schedule.

VERO LEWAND [*going up to* STARUSCH]:
   I've got to speak to you.

STARUSCH [*to* IRMGARD SEIFERT]:
   Unannounced, she invaded my apartment.

VERO LEWAND:
   This minute.

STARUSCH:
   That, unfortunately, is impossible.

VERO LEWAND:
   And I won't leave until you . . .

STARUSCH [*pointing to a chair*]:
   Make yourself at home. [*She sits down*]

VERO LEWAND:
   Why are you standing in Flip's way? Don't you see
   that he's got to do it? Without fail.

STARUSCH:
   Won't you take your coat off?

VERO LEWAND:
   I used to think you were a leftist, but now that
   you've softened up Flip, I know you're a reactionary
   —the kind that doesn't know it.

STARUSCH [*to* IRMGARD SEIFERT]:
   Please keep to the left! If I'm to the left of my dentist—right, Doc, you'll admit that?—then Scherbaum, unless he actually does it, is to the right of
   you, dear colleague—you, however, are not to the
   left of Vero Lewand, but where then?

VERO LEWAND:
   We demand that you leave Flip alone, as of now.

109

STARUSCH:

They'll kill him.

VERO LEWAND:

We demand a pledge from you in writing . . .

STARUSCH:

Philipp is no martyr.

VERO LEWAND:

Get this straight: I love Flip.

STARUSCH:

I hate confessions. I hate sacrifices.

VERO LEWAND:

Here's another Wednesday gone, and again nothing.
Now he wants to anaesthetize the dog. With injections. That'll ruin half the effect. You talked him
into it. You screwed him up. The guy's through.
Tells me he still doesn't know enough. All of a sud-
den he's got doubts. Maybe he'll even burst into
tears.

STARUSCH [*offering her a cigarette. To* IRMGARD SEI-
FERT]:

I admit it. I offered my student Vero Lewand a cigarette.

[DENTIST *enters*]

DENTIST:

The behaviorists regard smoking together as an attempt to check aggression. [*Exits*]

STARUSCH [*smoking also*]:

A filter cigarette.

IRMGARD SEIFERT:

The silly goose exhibited her duffel coat as a piece
of evidence.

110

STARUSCH [*to* VERO LEWAND]:
Wouldn't you rather take off your coat?

SCHERBAUM [*jumping up*]:
Careful, Old Hardy! Vero's going to crucify you.

STARUSCH:
Believe me. When I was seventeen, I too set my sights high . . .

SCHERBAUM:
I don't like her invading your pad.

STARUSCH:
But I'm a product of my years.

SCHERBAUM:
You've wasted enough time on me as it is.

STARUSCH:
I've adapted myself.

SCHERBAUM:
Because I can't make up my mind . . .

STARUSCH:
I was looking for a permanent compromise.

SCHERBAUM:
. . . and I'm a washout.
[*Sits.* VERO LEWAND *jumps up, throws herself on the Persian rug in front of the tables, wriggles*]

VERO LEWAND:
Actually, I don't think you're so bad, Old Hardy.

STARUSCH [*jumping up*]:
What is this nonsense?

VERO LEWAND:
It's comfortable here.

111

STARUSCH [*sits down*]:
  If you like the rug, don't mind me.

VERO LEWAND:
  It's great. Won't you want to join me? [*Wriggles*]

IRMGARD SEIFERT:
  Just imagine, Eberhard: The silly goose asked me.
  How do you like Herr Starusch's rug?

VERO LEWAND:
  Come on, Old Hardy!

STARUSCH:
  Just between you and me, Doc: The girl impressed
  me.

VERO LEWAND:
  Or can't you make it?

STARUSCH:
  I'll turn him on, she said. Then he'll leave you alone.

STARUSCH [*to* VERO LEWAND]:
  Be sensible, Vero.

VERO LEWAND [*jumps up*]:
  Really neat, your rug! [*To* IRMGARD SEIFERT]
  There. You see? His rug's fuzzy. Fuzz. Fuzz all over.
  Here, for instance. Fuzz all over . . .
  [*She laughs and runs off. The* DENTIST *enters*]

IRMGARD SEIFERT:
  What do you think of that?

STARUSCH [*pacing back and forth*]:
  And how are your zebra fish?

IRMGARD SEIFERT:
  Did you have a drink?

112

STARUSCH:

Are you able to imagine the academic consequences, Doc?

DENTIST [*laughs*]:

Coercions of dependents and minors. Headlines in
the illustrated paper: Pedagogy on Persian Rug!—
Teacher loves green panty-hose!
[*He exits.* SCHERBAUM *gets up, moves away from
desk*]

IRMGARD SEIFERT [*smiling*]:

Just imagine, Eberhard, the silly goose asked me
if I had ever lain down on your fuzzy Persian rug.
And yet, I like little Lewand. Her spontaneity ap-
peals to me. I had that same directness when I was
seventeen. Most of the time. Ultimately I'll still have
to step up in front of the class and unmask myself.
[VERO LEWAND *meets* SCHERBAUM]

SCHERBAUM:

Oh, come on. That doesn't count.

VERO LEWAND:

What about you, Flip?

IRMGARD SEIFERT:

Because what right would I have to find fault with
little Lewand's fibs if I myself continued, day after
day, to leave the truth at home.

SCHERBAUM:

I'll never make it.

IRMGARD SEIFERT:

I admit that I'm weak.

113

SCHERBAUM:

    I'll never make it.

IRMGARD SEIFERT:

    But once young Scherbaum sets the example, I'll overcome my weakness.

VERO LEWAND:

    If you don't do it, nobody will.

IRMGARD SEIFERT:

    He would have acted differently in our time.

SCHERBAUM:

    I'll really never make it.

IRMGARD SEIFERT:

    He wouldn't have quit.
    [IRMGARD SEIFERT *and* SCHERBAUM *exit*]

STARUSCH:

    I can't go on. Foretaste overlaps with aftertaste. Simultaneous tasting cancels itself out. I know what's in my pockets. Words interlock and open pigeonholes in which words lie waiting to interlock and open pigeonholes. I understand everything. Before the predicate enters and pompously occupies the stage, I'll nod: Yes, sir. Yes, sir.—Now I'm going to get some sleep. My rug measures twelve by sixteen.
    [*He lies down on the rug. The* DENTIST *enters and sits down next to* STARUSCH]

DENTIST:

    By the way, it's your turn again. Day after tomorrow.

STARUSCH:

No, Doc, no!

DENTIST:

Bridge replacements of missing teeth in the alveolar area require the grinding of six abutments.

STARUSCH:

I can't go on.

DENTIST:

You ought to learn from your student and entrust yourself to my care.

STARUSCH:

Tablets! Tablets! Or insensitivity accompanied by painful comprehension of all pain . . .

DENTIST:

Epicurus reproaches the Greek Stoics with apatheia, whereas Seneca, though an admirer of Epicurus, admits that he is sensitive to misfortune even if wisdom enables him to overcome every misfortune. But at the slightest toothache you reach for your tablets: Misfortune equals toothache.
[*He exits.* STARUSCH *jumps up*]

STARUSCH:

Isn't it conceivable that Nero, as a consistent student of Seneca, was driven by toothache to set Rome on fire? [*Takes two tablets*]

BLACKOUT

scene thirteen

[SCHERBAUM *in the dentist's chair.* STARUSCH *and*
VERO LEWAND *collide*]

STARUSCH:
  I didn't want *that.*

VERO LEWAND:
  You're gonna get something from me.

STARUSCH:
  I'm sorry, Vero.

VERO LEWAND [*slaps him*]:
  Just so you understand.

STARUSCH [*softly*]:
  I understand.

VERO LEWAND:
  That wasn't meant personally, just in general, by
  and large. [*She exits*]

DENTIST:
  Tartar removal is an a priori component of every
  treatment. [*To* SCHERBAUM] Now rinse.

STARUSCH [*next to his desk*]:
  And then what, Doc?

DENTIST:
  Then the prophylaxis . . . Unlike your teacher's

prognathism, your distal bite can still be corrected. [*He continues the treatment.* VERO LEWAND *enters with her bicycle*]

VERO LEWAND:

I'm going to sit on the café terrace. In the afternoon.

DENTIST:

They should have started with Philipp when he was four.

VERO LEWAND:

And I'll shovel in cake and ask for second helpings and go on shoveling it in. [*She jumps on the bike, rides in a circle*] Meringue shells with whipped cream! Black Forest cherry cake! Cheese cake! Almond crescents!
[*She exits.* IRMGARD SEIFERT *enters. Beside the aquarium*]

IRMGARD SEIFERT:

I should have taken better care of my tropical fish.

STARUSCH:

He's given up, by the way.

DENTIST:

A faulty analysis, my friend: He is renouncing direct action and turning to long-term tasks.

STARUSCH [*directly*]:

Well, my dear colleague, however complex our reactions to it may be, Scherbaum has thrown in the sponge.
[IRMGARD SEIFERT *to the couch*]

DENTIST [*to* STARUSCH]:

No! Certainly not! [*To* SCHERBAUM] Now rinse! [*To* STARUSCH] The young man's full of projects. He's taking the student magazine in hand. Informative articles. Black commentaries. Possibly manifestoes.

STARUSCH [*laughs*]:

Scherbaum the editor-in-chief!

IMGARD SEIFERT [*sits down*]:

So-called reason has triumphed again. Bravo!

STARUSCH:

Whom would you want to triumph?

IRMGARD SEIFERT:

Didn't I say bravo? Bravo.

STARUSCH:

You're disappointed, aren't you?

IRMGARD SEIFERT:

My little hobby will take my mind off it.

STARUSCH:

I suppose you expected Scherbaum to show the courage that you and I—yes, you too—lack?

DENTIST [*to* STARUSCH]:

Incidentally, your student said he didn't want to burn himself out with a single action and get to be like you . . . and keep on lamenting, like Old Hardy: When I was seventeen, I too . . .

IRMGARD SEIFERT:

And I had already decided to make a fresh start.

STARUSCH:

From scratch?

IRMGARD SEIFERT [*stands up*]:

I was going to stand up in front of my class, including Scherbaum, and read those terrible letters, sentence by sentence.—But it's no longer worth it. I give up, too. [*She exits*]

STARUSCH [*laughs*]:

Why so despairing? Donate the letters to Editor-in-Chief Scherbaum. He'll print them in the student magazine. Sentence by sentence. As a special feature, so to speak.

[VERO LEWAND *enters, rides the bike in circles around* STARUSCH *and tosses him a Mercedes star*]

VERO LEWAND:

Hi, Old Hardy. Want some? I used to do it with Flip. We called it picking stars.

DENTIST:

In the treatment of distal bite the following steps must usually be taken.

VERO LEWAND:

I'm gonna do something now.

DENTIST:

First the elevation of the bite . . .

VERO LEWAND:

I'm going to the terrace.

DENTIST:

Second, the retrusion of the upper front . . .

119

VERO LEWAND:

I'm going to eat cake. Lots and lots of cake!

DENTIST:

Third, the distention of the lower jaw . . .

VERO LEWAND:

Nut-cream cake!

DENTIST:

And fourth, the expansion of the upper jaw. [*To* STARUSCH] Your student will need patience.

VERO LEWAND [*disappointed and with exaggerated anger*]:

I'll just sit there and eat in protest. Everything that's expensive, spoonful by spoonful! [*Rides off*]

DENTIST [*to* SCHERBAUM]:

Rinse please!—That's why, and particularly in your case, the patient must be disciplined.

SCHERBAUM:

I'll stick it out, Doc.

DENTIST:

You'll have to live with the front plate for a whole year at least.

SCHERBAUM:

I'll stick it out.

STARUSCH:

We've pulled him through.

DENTIST:

It's the right treatment that counts.

STARUSCH:

Now he's an adult.

SCHERBAUM:

    I'll stick it out. Definitely, Doc, definitely.

    [SCHERBAUM *and the* DENTIST *exit.* VERO LEWAND
    enters]

STARUSCH:

    Tell me, Vero, is it a disaster?

VERO LEWAND:

    Not as bad as that if we carry on. And I *will* carry
    on. Look. [*Hands him a leaflet*]

STARUSCH:

    Exclamation points.

VERO LEWAND:

    Now things are really going to happen.

STARUSCH:

    Exclamation points all over.

VERO LEWAND:

    And no hemming and hawing.

STARUSCH:

    Too many exclamation points. No question marks.
    Not a single semicolon. [*Hands back the leaflet,
    exits*]

VERO LEWAND [*calls after him*]:

    Natch! It's too late for your semicolons. We got no
    time for semicolons. We're going to abolish your
    semicolons!

    [SCHERBAUM *enters*]

    . . .

121

SCHERBAUM:
We're having an editorial meeting. Will you join us?

VERO LEWAND [*after a pause*]:
No.

THE END